PLAYING WITH FIRE

Billionaire Playboys
Book 2

TORY BAKER

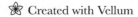

"If you want to heal your heart's wounds, start healing your thoughts." -Alexandra Vasiliu

ONE

Millie
_____

"Two black coffees, please, and a date with you tonight." Ezra walks in for the third day in a row this week. I have one AirPod in my ear, in which my best friend, Nessa, is talking about her plans with Parker this weekend and if I'm working or can take a day off work.

"Let me call you back. Some tall, handsome man in a suit is asking for coffee and a date." I wink at Ezra. He's in one of his expensive three-piece suits, hair slicked back in a way that tells me Four Brothers has him in meeting after meeting today. The two-day beard growth still shows off his jawline, darker than his hair color of ash brown with streaks of blond here and there. His gray eyes, though... Only three percent of the population has that beautiful color; I know because after meeting him, the first thing I did when there was a lull in customers was look it up, and they suck me into his vortex each and every time.

1

"We were together last night. Are you missing me already?" I ask after I hear the clicking in my ear telling me that Nessa hung up. Imagine our luck.— Parker and Ezra are best friends, and Nessa and I are best friends. Nothing could have prepared me for the coincidence when I received the call from my girl to tell me that when she took my place at her charity auction, who the winning bidder was. Getting sick never led to such great results before, because Nessa and Parker are conjoined at the hip, completely in love. As for Ezra and me, he's not there, but that's not to say I'm not.

"Is there a rule saying I can't have you in my bed every night of the week?" Ezra grumbles when I have to be up and at Books and Brews earlier than sunrise. I always suggest going home the night before or him staying in bed on the rare occurrences we make it back to my place. Ezra is a creature of habit; I get it, completely. The coffee shop I've been working at since college is that way for me. My small studio apartment, on the other hand, is also me—colorful, full of dark moody colors, outfitted with as many thrifted items I could find instead of polluting the earth with brand-new things when others are often getting rid of great stuff because it isn't on trend. What works for us may not work for others. I'm at Books and Brews starting at seven o'clock in the morning and not closing until three in the afternoon. The only snafu is the mornings —Ezra is not one to get up early if he doesn't have to.

"I didn't say that. Let me grab your coffees." The coffee shop is currently quiet for the time being; I know I've got about twenty more minutes before we'll be balls to the walls, chaos ensuing. If my barista no-call, no-shows today, I am going to be pissed. The owners of Books and Brews are now living on a white sandy beach in Florida. Their son comes in once or twice a month to look over the books on the computer, makes sure the shop isn't burnt to the ground, and that's about it. He doesn't want this place. I do, though, which makes it imperative that I keep it clean as a whistle, rolling in the black while also maintaining things running smoothly. So, I won't run to Bonnie, Chad, or even their son, Scott. I do what needs to be done on my own.

"What time were you thinking?" Ezra likes a pour-over, which takes a bit longer than pulling the lever in the pre-brewed coffee. This way makes it smoother yet stronger. I slide the two cups of coffee toward him after putting the lids on the to-go cups. If he were staying, I'd have given him the thrifted mugs we use. They're a dime a dozen, a reason for us to recycle, and when one breaks, we don't have to worry about the cost to replace it. I just find another mug when I'm venturing out to thrift stores on a Sunday, the only day we're officially closed.

"My last meeting is at six. I can pick you up around seven." What I thought was a slight wince clearly isn't. It's noticeable in the look he gives me. The last thing I want to do is close up the shop, clean, do inventory, drop off a deposit at the bank, then finally head home just to get dolled up. It's a Thursday evening, too, which means every place is going to have some kind of a wait even if it's not for reservations.

"Can we rain check on going out and stay in instead?" Ezra takes a sip of his coffee. I'm sure the other one is for Parker. Boston and Theo have yet to make their presence known here, and the only reason Parker has come in is because of Nessa.

"Yeah, my place or yours?" Ezra asks with a crooked smile, knowing what that does to me.

"Yours. It's closer to the coffee shop. At least this way, I won't have to get out of bed an hour earlier to get here on time," I answer.

"I like the way you think." I watch as Ezra leaves his drinks on the counter. The only other customer is in the other part of the shop, where we sell second-hand books.

"Ezra," I warn him not to do what he's about to do, but I'm unable to head him off with his tall, muscular body, watching as he makes his way around the corner until all that's left for me to do is turn toward him and prepare for the inevitable.

"Millie." Yep, nothing is going to stop him. His head dips down, his lips touch mine, and if I knew it was going to be a light peck, I'd have no issue. But that's not what Ezra is after, and he won't stop until he has his way. His hands grab my hips, pulling me close as his tongue sweeps across my lower lip, coaxing me to open for him, and there's no way I can refuse him. Not when my tongue meets his so willingly, allowing him to take over the kiss. My body is plastered to him, and we have a full-blown make-out session behind the counter at my place of work.

"Have a good day," he murmurs when our kiss ends, and like usual, he's leaving me wanting more. Ezra can work my body like nobody's business. I'm talking multiple orgasms. That big-dick energy of his is top notch, and even though he's currently heading out the door, he's also left me breathless, wet, and needy, all while I'm still in a stupor from only a kiss.

TWO

Ezra

"FINALLY." I WALK INTO THE MEETING ROOM, BOTH cups of coffee from Books and Brews in my hand, when Parker welcomes me by himself. Apparently, Theo and Boston won't be joining us. Millie's flavorful scent is still lingering on my body from how she plastered herself to me while I was taking her mouth, always so greedy the second I'm near.

"Where are the other two?" I ask Parker. I don't bother with pleasantries. He's my brother even though we don't share blood. What we share is thicker than any familial ties you could form—we both fought our way through our home life when we were kids, including each other. A fist fight, kids gathering around, each of us attempting to hurt the other with anything we could instead of feeling like we should. Parker made it less unscathed than me, healing himself. That's not the case with me. I come with baggage and beliefs that have people shaking their heads.

"Boston is out of town in New Orleans still. Not sure he'll be coming back anytime soon, if he has his way. Theo is running late, told me we'll catch up later. Is that my coffee?" I don't respond as I take the last sip out of my own, knowing that one isn't going to tide me over.

"Fuck, Boston may as well pack his shit and say goodbye to New York forever. I take it you did what he asked you not to and took the heat that his politician daddy was going to take out on his son. And no, you're not getting my coffee. Get your lazy ass out of bed earlier, hit the coffee shop, or make it yourself, or, if you're lucky, Nessa will make you a cup," I tell Parker as I take a seat to his left, grabbing the folder he placed in the middle of the table.

"Huh, is that the excuse you're going with? It's not because there's something else between you and Millie?" In all actuality, this cup was meant to be his. That's not happening now. One cup isn't going to do near enough to keep me awake and focused for the day since Millie wakes up earlier than anyone else I know, some of that her own doing, sometimes with her mouth wrapped around my cock. Other days, because she's doing the absolute most at Books and Brews, more than any other manager would, I'd say.

"I don't know what you're talking about." Playing dumb is better than admitting anything to my brother.

I know he'll throw the phrase *'What comes around goes around'* in my face. I'm no fucking idiot.

"So, you're saying I should call Mom, let her know that you and Millie are in a relationship, tell her to pop in tonight to meet her, kind of like you did to me?" Fucker. I see with that smirk and the arch of his eyebrow that karma is most definitely a bitch, and if I don't shut this shit down, his mom, my adopted mother, Krista, will most definitely make a trip into the city, use her key, and make herself known to Millie.

"Man, you're a bitch. Fine, take the coffee." I slide it toward him, a peace offering. Who knows if that will even work in my favor.

"Thanks. I knew you'd see things my way." Parker takes a sip of the black liquid, making a whole fucking production of it. While he does that, I open the portfolio while holding back the growl that's bubbling up inside of me. Millie is making me feel things that I don't want to talk about, think about, or see this early in the morning, or for the time being.

"Damn, that's good." Parker is poking the bear. It'll only give me more fuel for the fire once we're in the ring tomorrow morning.

"That's the one and only time. Now tell me what's going on with Four Brothers and Taylor and Associates," I urge.

"Paperwork is finalized. I've already signed it even though I wasn't supposed to be anywhere on this paperwork. Luckily, Nessa understands that it's impossible for me not to be. It's time for you and Theo to do the same. Boston came by the house last night to sign. A quick pit stop is what he called it before leaving immediately after. Next, we'll let PR handle the rest." Taylor and Associates is Nessa's father's company. Parker wanted nothing to do with the proposal, and I made sure that happened. This part, though, needed his name associated with it since Parker owns twenty-five percent of Four Brothers.

"Alright, I'll get this signed. I've got a meeting after this, then another later this afternoon." I take the pen, a Writers Edition Homage to the Brothers Grimm Limited Edition Mont Blanc, a gift from the asshole in front of me. It's gold and black, finely etched to perfection, gliding along the paper in swift smooth strokes, and then it's done.

"Sounds good. I'm heading home. If you need me, well, fuck off." You'd think Vanessa would have chilled his ass out. Yeah, right. If anything, he's more of a dick than ever, especially when it comes to not being around her.

"I figured as much. Later." We walk out of the board room, Parker going one way and me going the other. Some of us have to work in an office to actually get shit done.

THREE

Millie

TODAY WAS A DAY. NATURALLY, THE BARISTA WHO WAS scheduled never showed. It's a common occurrence with her. Instead of calling or texting, I made a note once again and carried on with my day. When everything was said and done, I was exhausted, barely making it from the coffee shop to the bank to deposit today's earnings, then stopping by my place, taking a quick shower, and packing a small bag before I took the subway to Ezra's place. He wasn't home. The doorman knows my name, and I have a key plus the code to his upscale condo, one that's two stories on the top of a very well-known building. That still doesn't stop me from texting him before entering the building.

> Millie: Hey, I'm at your place. See you soon.

I send the text right as Bill, Ezra's doorman, holds the door open for me to enter. I pocket my phone in my light jacket, unsure how we're having weather that's completely different than we're used to here in the city. It's flipped around, feels more like fall than the winter we usually experience, not a hint of snow and none in the forecast.

"Hello, Miss Millie."

"Hi, Bill. Please call me Millie. None of that *Miss* stuff." I scrunch up my nose, and he chuckles. "How's your day going?" No matter how many times I've told him over the past few months, he always includes it. At least he's no longer using my last name. It's not an easy name to spell, that's for sure.

"It's going better now that a pretty lady like yourself is in my presence. How about yours?" Ignoring me yet again, Bill is the consummate flirt, old enough to be my grandfather, and has a heart of gold.

"You're a sweet talker. Another two days, then I'm off of work, thank goodness," I tell him as he walks me toward the elevator, swiping the card across the panel to allow me up to Ezra's place.

"That's good. You work as hard as Mr. Hudson, and that's a lot." He is speaking a whole lot of truth on that subject matter.

"Soon, maybe I'll be able to slow down. Have a good night," I tell him as I step inside the elevator.

"You as well." My phone vibrates in my pocket. I took my AirPods out as soon as I walked into my apartment, giving my ears and head a break from the music I have playing or the phone calls I take, usually from Nessa, my grandmother, or Ezra. Now it's silence. There's no one in the elevator, and I'll have Ezra's place to myself for a few hours where I can decompress before having to sit down and figure a few things out. There's not even elevator music, and for that I'm thankful. I'd probably fall asleep standing up if there were. Instead, my mind runs in circles, thinking about the paperwork I have in my bag that I need to look over. I've wanted to buy Books and Brews or become a partner since the moment I stepped inside the shop. Going to college for business while working there made that feasible. Add in the side hustle of being an online stylist, and I've got a huge chunk of change in the bank. There is never a dull moment where I can sit and rest while I'm at the coffee shop, then, when I get home, it's time to put in another hour or so for my online work. Sure, my best friend and her parents would more than likely help me secure the loan, but I'd never accept that. I'd rather work my ass off to do it on my own than to feel like I owe someone else besides a bank. The what-if's would plague me every waking moment. My grand-mother, who raised me, has always been in my corner, tells me on the daily I'll accomplish anything I put my mind to. So, that's what I'm doing, although now it's going to be sooner rather than later. A year earlier than I wanted or expected. The money I have saved up is a lot. What sucks is there isn't enough, not in my eyes, and I'm worried it won't be in the bank's eyes either.

The elevator stops. I swipe my key card on the panel again. Yes, again, three times if Bill isn't at the front desk. Ezra's building is locked up tighter than Fort Knox. I step into the foyer. The living room is straight ahead as well as wrapping around the corner, leading to the terraces. If it were a bit warmer, that's where I'd be until Ezra comes home. Instead, I veer toward the right and head to the kitchen to put my bags on the table, giving myself the room to spread out and work on the documents. The owners of Brews and Books haven't mentioned selling since nearly seven or so months ago, but judging by the way their son has been by every month and the fact that I haven't heard from them besides through email, I'm assuming there's only a certain amount of time I have left. I'm placing my laptop bag on the chair, still having my overnight bag on my shoulder, when my phone buzzes again. I pull it out, figuring it's Nessa telling me something unimportant. A meme about the weather or how annoying men can be are par for the usual. A phone call is where the serious stuff takes place. It's not Nessa. I've got three messages from Ezra.

> Ezra: You don't have to text me every time you're at my place. See you for dinner.

> Ezra: Shit, looks like my meeting will be running late.

> Ezra: Chinese, pizza, or Japanese?

I have to smile at his rapid-fire texts. My phone going off was the least of my worries. All I wanted was to take my bags off my shoulders, get what's worrying me the most out of the way, and to relax for the rest of the night.

> Millie: I'll always text. It's rude not to. That's fine on the meeting. I have paperwork to do. And Japanese. I'll place the order when you leave, and you can pick it up on the way?

I put my phone down on the kitchen table, drop my overnight bag in another chair to put in Ezra's room later. An unspoken rule of his—sleepovers are allowed, but leaving things at one another's place is a completely different scenario. I wouldn't care if he left something at my house—a toothbrush, cuff links, a tie, but there is literally nothing, even after I offered to make room. Ezra shook his head, telling me no. I got the hint. His place is his place, and my place is my place. Did it sting? Absolutely. Am I glutton for punishment? Also yes.

> Ezra: Sounds good to me. See you later.

I don't respond, already know what we both like. Ezra is a creature of habit with all things, work, food, sleep pattern, and if I thought my past was screwed up, well, his gives me a run for my money. The reason my grandmother raised me would be because my parents were gone more than home, making our relationship even more strained. I chose to move in with my grandma at a younger age given the choice via my parents, her son and daughter-in-law, so she raised me, my parents sent money, and while I don't have a trust fund like a lot of my friends, I had plenty, enough to go to college without worrying. And I have a hefty amount in my high yield savings account. I know, I know, the smarter thing would be to put it in a CD, making me more in interest, but I wasn't sure when the time would come that I'd need to access the money. I grab my papers, laptop, and pen out of my bag, setting everything else aside, and then take my seat. It's time to get shit taken care of and make Books and Brews mine.

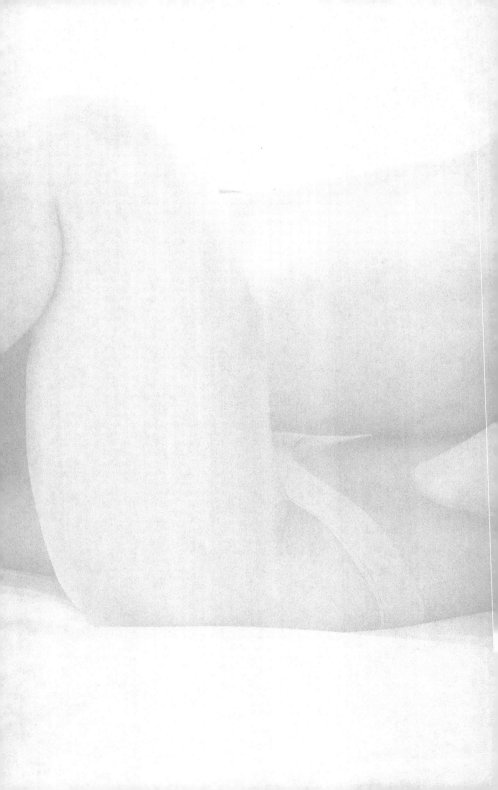

FOUR

Ezra

CHRIST, GETTING HOME CLOSER TO NINE O'CLOCK wasn't my idea of fun. The only good thing was walking through the door and seeing Millie sitting on the couch, a glass of white wine beside her and some reality trash television show on in the background. It's when she pops off the couch, rounding it, making her way toward me that the stress from the day falls off my shoulders. There is no way in hell we're making it to the bedroom. I take her mouth, nipping at her upper lip. A low whimper permeates the otherwise quiet living room. My tongue sweeps inside, getting another taste of her, a taste that never seems to last long enough. She matches me stroke for stroke. My hands grab her hips, pulling her closer.

"Ezra," she breathes my name between our kisses.

"I'm taking you, Millie. Bend over," I groan, backing away, taking my shoes, socks, suit jacket, tie, and buttoned-down shirt off quickly, leaving me in my undershirt and slacks.

"Is this how you want me?" I watch as she moves while taking my undershirt off with one hand at the back of my neck, hurrying so I don't miss a single fucking thing. The minute Millie arches her back, grabbing ahold of the arm rests, I'm on her faster than lightening flashing in a thunderstorm on a hot summer afternoon. All her soft flesh is on full display, that heart-shaped ass upturned, the glistening of her wetness coating the inside of her thighs.

"That's exactly how I want you." I step closer to her, just out of reach. My fingertips slide up the back of one thigh. "Spread, Millie." She does what I demand, so willing when I take her body with mine. I slide the tips of my fingers higher, coating them along the way until I'm right at her clit, fluttering them along her slit. Her body undulates. It has her reaching for more, going to the tips of her toes, searching for my fingers. The only reason I pull away is to deal with my belt.

"Ezra, hurry." She's always so ready and needy for my cock. I'm going to take my time with her tonight. Usually, I'd have her thighs wrapped around my head, eating until I've had my fill of her.

"Are you sure? I'm not going to go slow once I get inside of you," I tell her as I pull the condom out of my pocket. I keep a stash handy everywhere—my bedroom, the living room, the kitchen, the bathroom, and one on me at all times. Even with Millie being on birth control, I'm not willing to take that chance. I'm not at a place where children are anywhere near my future, if ever.

"I'm positive. Now get inside me." I slide the button through the hole, the rasp of the zipper giving away what I'm doing. That's when Millie looks over her shoulder, observing as my length comes into view. She licks her lips, and I remember exactly how she likes to suck me.

"Remember, Millie, you asked for it." I don't bother taking my pants the rest of the way off, just pull them down far enough to not restrain me. My hand wraps around my cock, the fabric of my pants rasping along the back of her thighs as I rub the fat tip of my dick along her drenched folds, waiting for her to respond.

"Damn it, Ezra, fuck me." I pull my hand away, grab both sides of her hips, and slam all the way inside her with one powerful thrust. Millie's cunt ripples around me. I can feel it through the latex separating me from feeling her completely. Some days, I curse myself over the fact that having children, or a wife, will never be a part of my future, but it's a necessary evil. Instead, I focus on not coming.

"Fuck, Millie, don't do that again." The clenching and unclenching of her tightness attempts to suck the willpower right out of me. I slowly slide out, the sensations taking root. My hands slide from her hips toward the front of Millie's body, one hand moving toward her clit, and as much as I'd like to take my time with her, that won't be happening this time around. Maybe the next round.

"Don't do this?" She moves her hips back while I'm sliding in and out, chasing my cock with her pussy. I swivel my hips as I work my way back inside her tightness, two fingers on either side of her clit working it while my other holds her tit, wanting as much of her in my hands as possible.

"Millicent." Her full name comes out. Her body tightens, making my balls jerk. We both love it from behind—her because my balls slap against her, and me because I can control her even when she thinks I'm letting her take over. I already know how I'll take her next—her straddling my lap, my body against the headboard as she rides me, her back toward me as I watch her ass shake with every upwards and downwards stroke.

"Ezra." I know that tone of her voice. She's on the edge. The one thing that will tip her over the edge is my ace in the hole, and I use it, dipping my legs, getting more momentum, using two fingers on her clit, rubbing it in a clockwise and then counterclockwise pattern.

"Get there, sweetness, now," I demand, knowing that if she doesn't come, I could potentially erupt before her, and that's not something I ever want to happen. Millie always gets hers before I get mine, no other way about it. Well, unless she's on her knees, my hands in her hair as I fuck her face, then all bets are off.

"Yes, Ezra, yes!" She explodes around me, her voice echoing through the entire bottom floor of my condo. Millie takes me over the edge in two more thrusts of my hips. I come inside the condom, and I don't stay planted inside her long either. As much as it sucks to pull out of her, it's better than fucking up. I pull out, holding the condom at the base of my cock.

"Do you need to stay there for a moment, or are you ready for round two in the bedroom?" I ask, noticing she's not moving. Her hair is still in a messy bun on top of her head, a few pieces falling out here and there, head tucked against the arm of the couch, chest heaving.

"Go away, Ezra. You're ruining my orgasm-induced euphoria." Her voice sounds soft and drunk. I leave her there to take care of the condom. If she's still bent over when I return, I'll help her out, even if that means carrying her to bed to get my fill of her.

FIVE

Ezra

"I HAVE TO GET UP," MILLIE WHISPERS WELL BEFORE her alarm is set to go off. I don't have to look at my phone or a clock to tell me she's unwrapping herself from my bed at least an hour earlier than her usual time, a time that is stupid o'clock.

"What the hell, Millie? Stay in bed." The palm of my hand curls around her lower abdomen beneath a borrowed shirt of mine. She's got nothing on beneath. We ate dinner in the living room last night, each of us enjoying our soup and sushi. Millie was sitting on the floor bellied up to the coffee table even though she knows I don't care if she eats on the couch. When she was finished with her food, picking at it like a bird, unlike me, who eats as if it's my last meal, she let out a soft sigh, moving until her back landed on the front of my legs. It wasn't long until I was tired of not having her closer to me. I spread my legs until her back met the couch, my head dipping down to whisper in her

27

ear. Her body shivered, and then I was standing up, collecting our trash, and making quick work of shutting down the house to get back to her. I no sooner got back to her than she was up on her feet, my shirt hitting her at mid-thigh, the TV was switched off, and my hand took hers. There was only one way to end the night, and that was balls deep inside of Millicent.

"I've got to finish going over my paperwork. I have a meeting, and my eyes were burning last night, so I couldn't finish it. Stay in bed." Letting her go is pissing me off, especially because I'm sure it's around five o'clock in the morning and neither alarm went off, meaning Millie probably didn't sleep a wink while I had no problem passing out after making her come four times to my two.

"I'm up now," I grumble. She lets out a breath, sounding frustrated when that's the last thing she should be. The woman doesn't stop moving, working at Books and Brews Monday through Saturday from sunrise to midafternoon, then working on her computer at another job. It seems the only time she's settled is when we're in bed, and even now that's not working.

"Ezra, you don't have to. I promise. Go back to sleep. This shouldn't take me long, and there's no reason for both of us to be up at this god-awful hour." I roll to my side, hitting the button on the wall near the bed to turn the lights in the room to low dim. No need to blind us while we're at it.

"Millicent, I'm already up. Do what you need to. I'll start the coffee and make breakfast." I'm still in bed, about to grab my phone. If I'm up this early, I may as well get some work done myself, and knowing my brother, Parker isn't up yet either, so there goes any idea of meeting at the gym to box my annoyance out.

"Don't *Millicent* me in that tone of voice. I gave you an out. You didn't take it. I'm going to change." She grabs her bag off the chair and heads to the bathroom. I hear the lock click into place. Message received, loud and clear. Though, I have no fucking idea what I've done to piss her off, and it's nowhere near that time of the month. Four months we've been together, not in a relationship—labels are unnecessary between the two of us—yet I know when it's that time. Millie's pussy is off limits, and no matter how many blowjobs she offers, or I receive, it's nothing like sliding in between her thighs.

"So, what has gotten into her?" I ask the now empty and silent bedroom. Figuring hanging out and waiting on Millie to get out of the bathroom is asking for more attitude than I'm prepared for, I head for the stairs. I'll be mainlining it today. I'm up two hours earlier than necessary, three if you count the fact that I'm not needed at the office till around nine. I walk through the house, turning on the lights as I make my way down the stairs and to the living room, grabbing the remote off the table behind the couch to turn off the room-darkening tint that is built into the windows. Once the sun starts rising, it'll let in the natural light. Until then, it's me, the coffee pot, and my dangerous thoughts. I toss the remote back onto the table then make my way to the kitchen in a few strides. The dining room is off the living room; it's never used unless Krista, the only real mom I've ever had in my life, demands we eat Sunday dinners here. And now Millie uses it more than anything—her laptop, file folders, and papers are spread around the whole surface. I don't usually look at her stuff. Normally, she's working her side job as a fashion consultant a few times a week, helping customers piece outfits together for a subscription box. The papers I'm looking at aren't what those are; it's loan papers for a staggering amount of money, and when I see a business proposal for Books and Brews, making sure to keep the name while bringing her own element into the fold, I don't know how to feel.

"Hey, sorry about that. I tried to be fast in the bathroom." My eyes leave the dining table and focus on Mille. Her back is ramrod straight when she sees what I've been reading.

"When were you going to tell me? I could be helping you. Jesus, Millie, you don't have to do this all on your own." The words come out cold and businesslike. I take her in. Her eyes show that fierce fire when she's pissed. She's in a white tee-shirt stretched across her tits with the name of the coffee shop emblazoned in black lettering, a pair of jeans that hit her low on her hips and are loose in the legs yet still give her shape.

"Why would I ask you for help, Ezra?" She crosses her arms beneath her breasts, hip cocked out to one side, foot tapping.

"I don't know, maybe because you know I'm in this type of business. Sure, I'm not a banker, but do you realize this would take a matter of minutes instead of the hours you've been pouring into it?" I've yet to change into clothes, not that I mind standing in front of her in nothing but a pair of loose pajama bottoms that I wear in the mornings. We both know the effect it has on us.

"Ezra, not to be a dick, but this isn't your business. You've asked not to put labels on this, and I've agreed to it. We don't even keep things at each other's places, your doing by the way. Therefore, I'm not putting you in the middle of what I want for my own."

"I see. Well, then I'll leave you to it." I walk out of the kitchen, giving her my back, heading to my office while seething at the fact that Millie is being stubborn. Another reason to not have a relationship. You go out and offer to help someone only for them to throw it in your face. Fuck this, and fuck that.

SIX

Millie
___

"WELL, THAT WAS A BUNDLE OF JOY TO DEAL WITH this morning," I say once Ezra is out of earshot. I was going to wake up early, let him sleep, get my work done, and then meet him back in bed. Clearly, those plans have been botched since Ezra has now locked himself in his home office. I gather my stuff. There's no use staying here when he's in a foul mood, and seriously, he has no reason to get mad. The man refuses to label this, saying we're not dating, we aren't in a relationship, basically friends with benefits, and there are times I've questioned myself about allowing this to go too far. The way he refuses to leave even so much as a footprint at my house. He knows I'm on birth control, too, which I mean, it's cool, he doesn't want kids, but damn if it doesn't sting that he doesn't trust me. And that's what it boils down to—there's no trust in this 'situationship'. It doesn't take long for me to gather my paperwork, laptop, and pens, stashing them back in my bag then moving it closer to the front door. I'm not sure what this means for Ezra and me. He acts like I've wounded his precious ego, and while maybe I did, it sure wasn't my intention. Stupid male pride. I walk up the stairs, light on my feet. The last thing I want to do is have another conversation with Ezra at the moment, not when my emotions are already all over the place. The ups and downs of my everyday life, socking my heart and soul into a coffee shop that I've wanted as my own could slip through my fingers at any time. Bonnie and Chad could decide to sell to a developer. It would sure as heck make them more money than the offer I'm writing. Then there's a chance Scott could sweep it right out from under me. It's hard to tell what could happen since they're a closed-off bunch, a huge change from before the owners left to retire in Florida.

I find a pair of socks in my bag. Thankfully, it's packed, and it won't take me long to slide them on before putting on my well-worn Birkenstocks. What can I say? Vanessa got me addicted to the shoes in high school, and now they've transitioned well into my thirties. When they do finally break, I have no issue replacing them. I'm grabbing my bag while remaining as silent as a mouse as I head back down the stairs, which is hard to do in a shoe with zero support on your heel.

Maybe this is the beginning of the end. There are so many variables. I mean, the last time, I was sick—which is also when my best friend got together with Ezra's best friend. The only time I heard from him was a text here or there. Meanwhile, Parker pulled out all the stops to win Vanessa. The same can't be said for Ezra. Nope, that man has his mind, body, and soul locked up. I stop right outside his office door, hand pressing against the solid dark walnut-colored door. I hold firm in my stance to not poke the bear. "Bye, Ezra." A small silent farewell is what I give him instead. Who knows if I'll be back, and I can't waste time wondering when the paperwork in my laptop bag is calling my name. I'm only hopeful that Bill or his nighttime replacement is down in the condo lobby. The train station is going to be packed, and a taxi will more than likely be impossible to find. Jesus, today is really shaping up to be a pain in my ass. I grab my other bag and hit the elevator button to carry me downstairs, wondering if I should have left my keys on the foyer table while I was at it. That will have to wait. Ezra has his key to my place, and I'm not going to turn around and walk to his office to ask. Too bad Vanessa isn't working nights this week. I could really use her to talk me through this disaster of a morning.

SEVEN

Ezra
___

I HEAR THE DOOR TO THE ELEVATOR DING, SLIDING open, and then closing. My head tips back against my office chair, struggling if I should have hung up the emergency phone call my mother just hit me with as soon as my ass met the chair.

"Don't stress out, boys. It's only a small bruise to my head. I'm only calling you and Parker as a courtesy," Mom says on our three-way call I wonder who taught her how to use that capability. I'm sure it was someone at the church daycare where she works.

"I swear to God, between you and Vanessa, I'm never going to breathe fully again. Tell us again what happened," Parker demands.

"I'm not stressed. *Concerned* and *worried* are the words that come to mind." Which I am. She lives in a different part of New York than where we are, refusing to leave the area and move closer. No matter how much we ask, offer, or bug her, she refuses to. Stubborn through and through and independent a mile long. Parker chose a woman like Krista in every way, shape, and form. It seems I may have as well if I can fix us that is.

"Whatever. I'm not stupid. If I so much as scratch my arm, the two of you are ready to take apart whatever table I bumped into. This was all on me. I was making a bottle for the nursery, didn't close the overhead cabinet after I dropped something, and when I stood up, I hit the corner of it, and it didn't move back. A few staples, a day or two rest, and I'll be good as new," she says like this isn't a big deal.

"Excuse me? Did you say *staples*? Jesus, Mom, we're on our way. You're coming back with either me or Ezra, your choice, but it's happening," Parker demands. That's going to fly over like a turd in a punch bowl, in five, four, three, two, and one.

"Parker Matthew Hudson, that is enough. I'm staying home. If you three want to come up this weekend, I'd love that. Now, Ezra, talk to me. You're never silent, and you are this morning." I'm upset, not only with Mom and the situation, because I'm not stupid, and neither is Parker. She more than likely has a concussion. What other reason would she rest at home for, at her own will?

"I'm fine. Are you going to tell us everything, or am I going to have to resort to bribing your doctor or hacking into the hospital's data base?" Mom laughs, then whines in pain.

"Parker, Hudson, neither of you are doing anything of the sort, okay? I'm under concussion protocol, but that's more for workman's comp than anything else. I'll call if I start to feel off," she's appeasing us, plain and simple. Parker is already letting out a breath of air, pacified by what she's saying. "Plus, I am not going to be a third wheel in your house, and I'm not stupid, Ezra Hudson; you're quieter, not joking around like your usual self. I'll give you today to collect your thoughts. After that, I'm in full mamma bear mode, you hear me?"

"Yes, Mother," I chuckle, even though it's dry as a bone. Between Mom and Millie, my mind is fucked.

"Yeah, Ezra, when are you going to tell Mom about the girl in your life?" Parker tacks on. "Payback's a bitch, baby brother." He's older than me by a few months, the cocksucker.

"Well, considering she's no longer here, there may not be much to say, and yeah, we'll see about who's paying whom back when I have your ass in the ring." Admitting that to these two is only going to fuel their fire.

"Ezra, stop cussing. Parker, quit instigating. On that note, I'm getting off the phone. We all know you boys can track my whereabouts down, so do that. I'm going home. Seems the only person I'll be listening to is a handsome older doctor, and yes, I gave him my number. Love you boys." The phone clicks, leaving Parker and me on the line.

"Did she just say what I think she did?" Parker asks.

"Fuck, I need coffee or whisky, maybe both, and yeah, it seems Mom is finally putting herself on the market. "I wish the dude good luck. Between the two of us and mom, the guy may run for the hills before the first date is over," I reply.

"You're not wrong. Care to figure out who her doctor is and do a little digging?" We both have a guy on hand for this. My hacking days are over for the most part, The government doesn't take too kindly to that type of thing. When you're a teenager and under the age of eighteen, sure, but at my age, there's too much to lose.

"I have Kurt on standby. If Mom catches my hand in the honey pot, we're fucked." I run my fingers through my hair, wondering what the fuck I'm going to do about Millie.

"Good idea. Hey, Ezra?" Parker gets my attention.

"Yeah."

"You need me in the ring, say the word." I don't respond because like mother, like son, the fucker hangs up the phone. It seems everyone besides myself has something to do. I get up, put my phone in my pocket, and walk toward my closed door, cursing up a storm. If only I hadn't shut the door, Millie probably wouldn't have left. It would at least have allowed me time to ask for another moment. A fucking do-over is what I need, and a game plan. I walk out of my office, noticing the emptiness and quietness of my place. It's damn palpable. There's no television playing softly in the background, no tapping away at keys or scratching of paper when Millie makes notes in her planner, and there certainly aren't any sounds in the kitchen. The only thing I'm left with is the soft scent of a woman who I was an arrogant prick to.

"Coffee, then fix this shit, Ezra," I tell myself, unsure how I'll ever be able to make this right. Allowing her to leave a few things here, or for me to keep some at her place, is an easy fix. It's the wanting a relationship that is worrisome. My biggest fear is getting close to Millie and not being able to give her everything she wants. She will grow resentful of me when I don't want a family. Then what? Then she hates me, that's what. "Fucking fuck." I place my hand on the kitchen counter, not knowing how I even got to where I am. Today is going to be one of those days, one where I'm not stepping foot in the office. There's no way my mind will be on work, and the last thing I need is to fuck up a contract. Parker, Theo, and Boston would never let me live that shit down.

EIGHT

Millie

"I'LL SEE YOU MONDAY AT FOUR O'CLOCK, MILLIE," the banking consultant, Perry, who is on the other end of the line, tells me. I've been talking to him about this for the past six years. He's more of a friend than my banking consultant. Hence why were more on a first name basis. Plus, given my last name is not easy to pronounce, let alone spell—Millicent Saoirse—it's easier. If people were to take the time to listen the first time, they'd know it's Ser-sha.

"Thank you again, Perry. I know this isn't the normal time frame, and I truly appreciate you fitting me in." I called two days ago, asking if I could get my business plan together. When Perry, knowing from our prior meetings along with my finances, told me it might take a few weeks, I almost balked. Scott's last time coming into the coffee shop was way more awkward than before, and the emails are getting less and less

43

frequent, which is okay, except now they don't ask any questions, which is completely unlike them.

"Not a problem. It's been a long time coming. You've been talking about opening your own place one day since you walked into my office with your first thousand dollars to put in a savings account." Doing it on my own was the only way, so that's what I did. I scrimped and saved as much as I could for as long I could. Where my best friend had a trust fund or her parents to help her out, my parents weren't wealthy like that. Nessa wouldn't take their money regardless. The only thing she used them for was a place to live during her college years, plus a few things for her apartment, and I'm pretty sure she's still not touched the trust. I don't begrudge her. I love how fiercely independent she is, which is why the first time I mentioned buying Books and Brews from Bonnie and Chad, and Nessa asked me if I wanted any help, I shut her down before the sentence was finished. She got it. We both needed to do our own thing without money from others.

"That seems like a lifetime ago." I'm at the shop now, having finished the preliminary paperwork in a hurry once I finally made it home, pushing my personal drama to the side. One thing I've learned in my thirty years of life is that the only person you can depend on is yourself. No one else is going to do life for you.

"Maybe so, but the memory is still the same. You were so proud of the tips you'd been saving from Books and Brews. I hadn't seen anyone with so much pride in a long time, Millie." Perry is older, sixty or so, and the only man I trust with my money, since that thousand dollars is closer to a hundred thousand now after he convinced me to move things throughout the years, only keeping it out of savings and lockouts until I told him that it was time.

"All the same, thank you. I appreciate everything you've done. I'll have the rest of the paperwork ready to bring with me," I tell him. Sasha, one of the two baristas we have here, is working the counter, which allows this conversation to take place. If the shop were busy and I had no back-up, an AirPod would be in my ear at all times, taking calls for the shop, listening to my best friend, or having music playing softly. Is it professional? Probably not. Does it keep me sane? One hundred percent.

"See you soon." We hang up. Another nervous burst of energy settles in the pit of my stomach. There's still so much to get done today—payroll, ordering supplies, setting up a schedule that will undoubtedly get screwed up by Tasha. Yep, Sasha and Tasha, one who never misses a shift and another who never comes in. The worst part is they're sisters. Night and day, that's what they are. I take my AirPods out, put them back in the case, and place it next to my phone. In order to do inventory, I need complete silence. Math is not my favorite part, and having to count all the to-go cups, lids, syrups, and coffee itself, not even starting on the creamers and sugars, is a task in itself. Thankfully, the book part of the store is easy, mostly dealing with donated books from others, charging a few dollars compared to prices for brand-new books, and what we do charge is to help with overhead. Literally, Books and Brews makes hardly a dollar on every book sold. Another part of my business plan is to hold an open mic night, maybe a few signings from authors who wouldn't mind bringing in books to be signed. It's all part of a bigger plan.

I get in my zone, even when my thoughts want to linger on a certain gray-eyed pain in my ass. I refuse to deal with his hot and cold behavior. You can't have it both ways, or perhaps I'm lying to myself, and you can. Maybe I'm the problem after all. Wouldn't that be the kicker? It's not like I've used my words recently with the man. Something changed. At first, it was easy —sex, friendship, cut and dry. Somewhere along the way, I caught feelings, and now I'm the one holding a grudge because of his past.

"Hey, Millie, sorry to interrupt, but the espresso machine is making that weird grinding noise again, and I know you were able to fix it last time." I was jotting down a few things when Sasha walked in.

"Hey, no problem. It probably has grinds stuck in it again. Are there customers waiting on it?" I ask, dropping the clipboard and pen on the shelf in the back room.

"Yeah, I was making a triple espresso when it started." I follow her out. Last time was an easy fix; a thorough cleaning after the day was over seemed to do the trick. I'm hoping it'll be the same today. But with customers waiting and only one machine working, things could get tricky during the lunch hour when people stop by for an afternoon pick-me-up.

"Crap, alright. I'll help get the line down, then work on it. We may be down to one machine for the time being, though." I make a mental note to call the company to have a repairman come. As expensive as these machines are, the warranty is an absolute must. No way can we go a full day without two machines.

"Thanks, I appreciate the help. I know this will put you behind."

"It's not a problem at all. Just remind me about that when my knees are on the counter, aching from dealing with the machine," I joke with Sasha, making a mental note to give her more hours as well as a raise if I can finally make Books and Brews mine.

NINE

Ezra

TWO PHONE CALLS, THREE TEXTS. I'D SEND AN EMAIL if I thought Millie would respond. As it stands, everything has gone unanswered. That was an hour ago, the amount of time it took me to finish up with a few work things then get here. Fucking traffic is a nightmare on a Friday afternoon. It's a good thing I'm as close as I am to Millie's shop. I couldn't imagine how long it'd take from Millie's place, not to mention the construction that's never ending.

I open the door. The chime rings to announce someone has entered, except it's too busy right now to be heard over the cacophony of people talking, music playing, and the whir of coffee machines that are constantly running. My eyes glance over the entirety of the store, looking for Millie. To the right is a room filled to the brim with books, well, as many as they can store in the small four-hundred-square-foot place.

An arch entrance keeps it open and airy, since the only window in the place is in the front of the building. Every chair and table is currently occupied. Books and Brew is fucking booming. It's been around for nearly twenty years, but only the last ten has it really become more popular. The owners know that, and so do the people in the area. Millie buying this place will be nothing short of amazing. Hopefully, she'll add touches of her own, maybe cut back on hours here and there, have more of a staff that's reliable. I pan my view back around, noticing a barista is hustling back and forth from the cash register to the machine. An ass I'd know anywhere is moving in the air, one I've had in my hands, in my lap, my fucking mouth when I'm nipping at the globes when she gets mouthy. What I don't understanding is what exactly Millie is doing. I make my way through the people, tables and chairs set up here and there, dodging with their coffee in hand leaving the shop. My sole focus is on Millie. Her leaving today, Krista being hurt, it had me reeling. Things suddenly became clearer. I'm not saying that I'm ready for the "L" word; there are a shit ton of things I still need to iron out. What I do know is that I made a mistake this morning, going on the defense when I should have been playing offense all along. Attacking a woman when she's already on the edge was fucking stupid. I've got an apology to make and a woman to soothe.

I'm behind the counter, right behind Millie, sick and tired of the men in this place watching a show that isn't theirs. "Millicent, please get down from there." I don't use the word *please* very often. Since I'm already on her bad side, picking her up off the bar and placing her on her feet would only end in her yelling and screaming, a scene neither of us need.

"I'm almost done. This stupid thing. The grinds keep getting stuck. I think the blades need to be sharpened, which means I'll have to wait on a freaking repairman." My hands go to her hips, holding her steady as she wiggles down off the counter. The show she was unknowingly giving is over, thank Christ. I don't breathe a sigh of relief until both of her feet are planted on the ground, my hands still on her curvaceous body.

"Are you okay?" Her signature hair style when she's at work or relaxing after a shower is up in a bun. This time, it's falling down more than usual, almost as if she's been so busy today that it hasn't occurred to her to adjust it like I know she does.

"Yes, no, maybe. This is getting annoying. I have no one but myself to rely on, and while that would be well and fine if I made an owner's salary, I'm not. Plus, Bonnie, Chad, or Scott not responding is making me ready to pull my hair out." There's a forlorn look on her face, which has me thinking the worst. Did she already hear back from the bank? Is her dream going up in smoke? And if so, how can I make her dream a reality? I could offer her the money, but that won't work. Millie would never accept. I could buy the building from the bank. Underhanded, but it's a definite option. The place could go up for rent. The loan amount I saw on the application with what she's putting down as a down payment, that is another idea.

"Sasha, do you mind if I steal Millie for a few minutes?" I ask the barista. The line has died down a lot. The lunch crowd is happy now that they have coffee, and them not sticking around to watch Millie's shapely ass wiggling helps, too.

"Not at all."

"Come on, sunshine." I take her hand. She doesn't pull away from me, a good point in my book seeing as how I fucked up royally only six hours ago.

"Ezra, we have to make this talk quick. I can't leave Sasha up there with one espresso machine, try to get ahold of the owners, then call in an emergency repair order, and still do inventory." Son of a bitch, Millie's got shit piling up on her.

"You've been doing this forever. Take a deep breath," I tell her once we're in the small back office that also houses all of the inventory. It's a tight fit. Most businesses are in this district, where the majority of the blueprint is being used for the store. The back is an afterthought.

"You're right. Shit, I hate when you're right." I chuckle as she composes herself.

"Okay, you email the owners, then go back out front to help Sasha. I'll call the repairman and do inventory." Millie nods in response, already heading toward the desk chair. If I think what happened this morning isn't bothering her, too, I'll be sorely mistaken. I also know it's coming. There's a storm brewing, and it's aimed right at me.

TEN

Millie

WHAT A SHIT SHOW, LITERALLY AND FIGURATIVELY. Even with Ezra's help, it still took longer to place the order for restocking. The line finally died down, but where yesterday, we were hustling people in and out, today, it took a bit longer. A blessing in disguise. More books were sold while they were waiting on their coffee. The good news is, Ezra worked his magic, so someone is coming out for the espresso machine today. The bad news is, he won't be able to get here till well past closing time. It put me in a bind, massively. Sasha left when her shift ended, leaving me on my own, well, minus Ezra, who somehow isn't working today and has been here the entire time, giving me whiplash.

"Crap," I grumble. Still no email from Bonnie or Chad. Scott isn't answering anything either. Who the hell does this? Books and Brews is a business, not an outfit you wear once, throw in the laundry basket, and forget about until you get to it.

"Go to the bank. I'll stay here. Justin, the repairman, probably won't even arrive on time. You should be back before he gets here." Ezra comes up behind me. I've got the deposit bag in front of me, my front leaning against the counter, holding steady with one foot planted on the ground and the other on the inside of my knee in a triangle pattern. I've done this since I was a little girl, balancing myself on one foot, except with the presence of the man behind me, the counter is helping me more than normal. Ezra's thumbs and hands work magic along my neck, massaging the worry, stress, and annoyance away even though he's part of the equation.

"If you keep doing that, I won't go anywhere, and I'll be a pile of goo." One of these moments, we're going to have to confront what happened this morning, and since I'm being a chicken shit, it clearly won't be me.

"I've got no problem massaging the trouble away." Ezra's whisper carries along my ear, doing nothing to calm my nerves, heightening a completely different issue. "And as much as I don't want to break the calmness you've got going on right now, we need to talk about this morning." My eyes slam shut, unsure how to navigate his statement. I take a deep breath and hold it in, probably longer than any healthcare worker would suggest. But it works, even though I'm seeing stars. I'm taken to a calmer place in time, then finally let it out once I can't hold it in any longer. I do it one more time while Ezra's hands move from my neck and shoulders until his arms are wrapped around my upper chest, stepping closer to me, blanketing me in his heat.

"Please don't ruin the moment, not right now. I can only handle so much, and I'm right at the edge of my breaking point." That cliff people talk about, being on the edge, where all you can see is the cavernous ruin, when you're stepping back as much as you can, but the edge keeps disappearing, that's me exactly right now.

"Alright, we'll talk about it later. I will tell you this: I'm either at your place, or we're at mine, none of this going to bed angry or without one another." Never in all my years would I not confront someone who's made me re-evaluate my personal life. I am today mainly because I'm not ready to say goodbye to Ezra. Also, I just can't handle the mental and emotional upheaval.

"It'll have to be my place tonight. I have paperwork to go through, a meeting with my bank on Monday, plus my bag isn't packed or with me." Usually I'd pack for the weekend, not going home until Monday. That won't be happening this weekend. Tonight, I want to do some research on costs for how I'd like to improve Books and Brews and make it my own; the name isn't trademarked or anything, so if Bonnie and Chad allow it, I'll be able to keep it. What I'd love to do is have light wood built-ins added in the bookstore section. I'm talking floor-to-ceiling with a ladder on each side. Plus new couches, olive green and velvet in fabric. Throw pillows that have orange and mustard yellow tones. The walls all need to be repainted, too; the white walls are a glaring contrast to the orange-ish wood tones they've got going on now. I've got several boards online and magazine cut-outs of ideas. If I can buy it as is, make the changes slowly on the one day a week we're closed, it won't take long at all. The built-ins would take the longest, and even then, it'll be worth t.

"That's fine. Why don't we do this. We'll both wait for Justin. Once he's done, we'll go to the bank together. Then grab some food to cook at your place, and I'll stay the night." Ezra's solution works. The only reason I usually drop the deposit off during daytime hours is for convenience, ease, and in my mind, it's safer. I don't know why I think the way I do; criminals don't have a set of hours to abide by or anything.

"Alright. Not sure what you're going to wear home tomorrow, but I have a spare toothbrush." Sweep it under the rug, Millie, why don't you.

"I'll wear what I've got on. Appreciate the toothbrush, sunshine." He kisses the top of my head, and I bury my head in the sand, unwilling to even think about how things are going to go when we finally confront the issue.

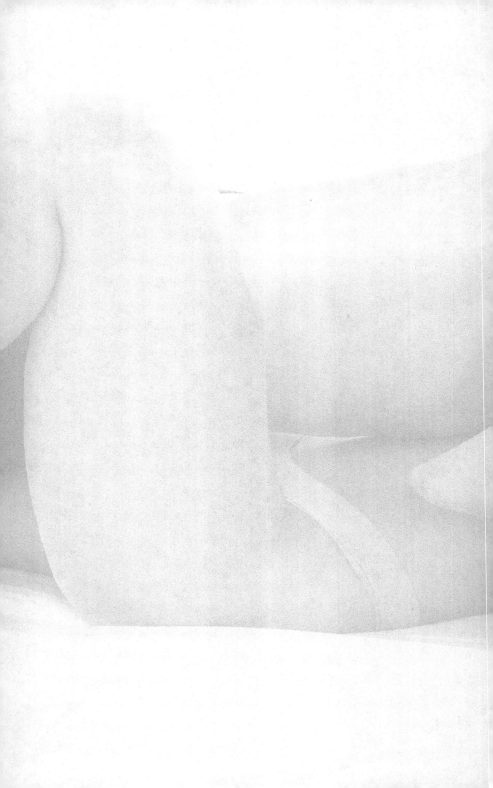

ELEVEN

Ezra
___

THIS MORNING WHEN MILLIE WOKE UP, IT WASN'T before her alarm clock. She hit the snooze three times, each time rolling back over and snuggling deeper into my side. After Justin arrived, he took the espresso machine apart and repaired it, which in fact did need new blades to grind the coffee beans. A true smile was plastered on Millie's face, basically an 'I told you so' without saying the words. That settled her down some, the stress from the machine being fixed. My driver stopped at the bank for her to do the deposit, then at a store to pick up a few items to cook dinner, and then we were at her place. It was nearly eight o'clock when we walked through the door to her apartment. I offered to cook our dinner, one of those take-and-bake meals, easy for a night when you're dog fucking tired. Millie was slowly crashing. Dark circles appeared beneath her eyes, the slope of her shoulders sinking, so I sent her to grab a shower while I prepared our meal.

"Millie, sunshine. You've got to get up, unless you're calling out of work." I graze her forehead with my lips, my fingers pulling up the shirt she's wearing, one of mine she must have snagged, while I'm trying to find skin.

"I can't call out of work. It's not like anyone else would show up," she says groggily. I did what Millie asked, not so much as bringing up yesterday morning, even if the need to apologize is only making me feel even guiltier.

"Then you get ready. I'll make coffee and breakfast, and call Mike to take you to work, then I'll head home." Missing work yesterday has me behind on emails and phone calls, undoubtedly so. I also need to call Parker and get my ass in the ring. I already know what he'll say, the same thing Krista has told me from the time she formally adopted me. I'm not a product of my past. Too bad my psyche won't allow me to let shit go. Forgiving and forgetting is damn near impossible when you're dropped off at a foster home at the age of eight, half-starved, dirty, and in need of more than what you're provided with by a family who only sees you as a paycheck. All because your mom was chasing a high, couldn't afford you and her habit. A father who was never around; she never spoke a word about who or where he was. I was another kid who got lost in the system until I met Parker.

"Yes, God, yes. That sounds better than sex right about now." I chuckle, moving us until Millie is on her back, her thighs spread open as I work my way between them.

"Is that so? Better than my cock or my mouth, too?" Her hair has fallen out of her bun, the brownish red strands tumbling around her shoulders, eyes still drowsy with sleep, a soft smile playing on her face.

"Hmmm, when you put it that way, maybe not?" I'm on my elbows, caging her in on either side of her head. Her legs move to wrap around my waist, and I move my hips, my cock hitting her bare pussy. I didn't bother putting any clothes on when we came to bed. Millie wasn't in the headspace for sex, and I wasn't going to push it. That still didn't mean I was wearing boxers. Never have and never will.

"If we had more time, I'd make you eat those words, sunshine. As it is, you'll barely make it to the shop on time." I drag the underside of my cock along the slit of her pussy, feeling her legs tighten around me, knowing with one dip of my hips, I'd be inside her, nothing between us. And as much as we both want that, time isn't on our side. Neither is the fact that we've yet to talk, and sex is only going to cloud her head more.

"Tease, that's what you are, Ezra Hudson." She doesn't pull away. I rock my hips a few times until her slickness is coating my length. I'll keep her scent with me the entire fucking day.

"You're right about that, but I'm teasing myself, too, Millicent. Now, go get ready for work. I don't want you stressed out. When you're through, I'll pick you up, and you can choose where we land. Tomorrow is your day off. I'm extending my hand to help with the business plan. It's there; what you do with it is up to you. We'll talk more after, though, okay?" Millie moves her hips, notching her cunt right on the head of my cock. My head drops, chest tightening with every deep breath.

"Here this weekend. I like your place, Ezra, but everything is here, and it'll be easier. After my appointment Monday, we'll talk, figure things out, and see where we go from there." She doesn't move any closer, but she doesn't pull back either.

"That'll do. You're playing with fire, sunshine." A part of me wants to say fuck it, thrust in, feel her without anything between us. I know myself. I'd not leave her body, not until she came, and then she'd suck the cum right out of me, repercussions be damned.

"Me? Turnabout is fair game." My mouth presses against hers, tongue licking her lower lip, which causes me to push inside of her.

"Christ, we're coming back to this, and soon," I tell her after our kiss is over, pulling away. My cock is none too happy with me. Neither am I, damn it.

"Okay." Millie is just as breathless as I am, and damn if that doesn't do something to me.

"Get ready. I'll make you coffee and breakfast to go." I slide out of the bed, grab my boxers off the floor, put them on, and head to the kitchen. My head is a fucking mess, and the only way I'm going to clear it is in the ring with my brother.

TWELVE

Millie
___

TRUE TO EZRA'S WORD, HE SAT DOWN ON MY LIVING room couch, papers spread around us, my vision board in full view. The two of us got after it once we woke up this morning, a heaviness still in the air between us from Friday morning. One more day, that's all there is left until I bring everything with me to the bank.

"Do you want ice?" I ask. He came to pick me up, showing up at Books and Brews after closing hours and helping me do the tasks like he did the day before. The difference was when he left my apartment that morning and returned to me that afternoon, it was with a bruise around his eye and a few forming along his chest.

"No, I'm okay," he responds as he looks at my final proposal, making notes on a sticky pad in the margins. My nerves are eating me up inside. How I'm going to survive the rest of the night and work tomorrow is anybody's guess. I only hope I don't take someone's head off because I can feel it boiling inside me, like a pot of boiling water on an unwatched stove, slowly creeping over the edge unless you turn it down. Even then, I'm not sure that would calm my ass down. "Millicent, breathe, sunshine. This is good, really freaking good. A few tweaks here and there; totally optional, by the way. You've got the money, the vision, and the experience. I don't know what your credit score or debt-to-income ratio is, but I'm willing to bet it's rock fucking solid."

"Are you sure? I mean, I have one or two credit cards. They get paid off monthly. Rent, phone, power, the usual. So, my credit score should be good. You see where I live, but the rent is still freaking steep. And are we going to talk about the fact that you're black and blue? Friday is still up in the air, and I feel like we're in this weird stalemate of a situationship, and I'm floundering. There. I said it. I can't take it anymore." Nessa told me that sitting on this was a bad idea. She was right, because here I am, a damn mess, an ache deep in my chest. I want it so much to work in my favor, worried that the other shoe is going to drop.

"Parker and I fought it out. You think I'm a mess, ask Nessa how he's doing," Ezra jokes. My humor is gone. Him not touching on the other stuff only causes my worry to deepen. He must notice, since he places the pen down, stands up, and moves toward me. While he was reading over everything, I couldn't sit in one place, so pacing the floor it was. "Millicent, I'd have apologized earlier, and I should have. I'm giving it to you now. I'm sorry, so fucking sorry. I am and have been a complete and utter dick, Friday being the worst. I didn't handle that well. You're one hundred percent right. We've got things to discuss. I've got shit to work through, which I'm doing. I'm asking for time until we can label this. You deserve more, I know. I'm a bastard for even asking you that, believe me, I know. Until then, I want you to leave clothes at my place, and I'll do the same here, okay?" I shouldn't be alright with what he's saying. I should demand more, but his life wasn't like mine, and while having absentee parents still stings, grandma Rose was there. He had no one until Parker and Krista came along. What he had before that wasn't a childhood; it was survivorship. I nod, understanding and forgiving him for Friday all at once. "What I can tell you is that a life without you, Millicent Saoirse, is no life at all."

"Oh, Ezra." He stops right in front of me, his hand cupping my neck, the other going to my hip, holding me in place, stopping me from pacing. I see the genuineness in his face, hear it in his tone, and feel it in the way he's holding me.

"Are we good now?" he asks. My heart is in my throat. No one has ever said anything like that to me, not with the depth and meaning Ezra did.

"We're good., I'm sorry too. I have so much going on, and instead of talking about it like a grownup, I let it fester inside me until I blew up. That wasn't fair to you either." I'm now going to have to tell Nessa she was right. I'll never hear the end of it.

"You've got not one single thing to apologize for. My past is fucking with my future. I'm going to work on that, this time for good." He gets the words out before I attack him, my lips on his, sighing at the feel of him taking over the kiss, tongue sweeping inside, tangling with mine. Ezra's hands delve beneath my hair, holding me right where he wants me. My hands are uncontrollable, though. A master at multi-tasking, they go to the waist of his lounge pants and slide inside, wrapping the palm of my hand around his thick and heavy length. It's been days since he's been inside me, and I'm ready to feel him again.

"Millie." He pulls his lips from mine, a hunger in his eyes, and I know he wants me as much as I want him.

"This is what I want, Ezra, so much. It's been too long," I admit, my wrist twisting with every upward and downward glide along his cock.

"Fuck, yeah." My hand is off his length, body wrapped around his as he picks me up by the cheek of my ass, literally one-handed, legs wrapping around his tapered waist, and I know we're going to have the best time making up for lost time.

THIRTEEN

Ezra

THIS GRAND IDEA OF MEETING MILLIE BACK AT THE coffee shop isn't going to happen. It leaves me with one ace in the hole, asking her to spend the night at my place.

> Ezra: Hey, you good with staying at my place tonight?

> Millicent: Sure. I might be late getting there. I don't know how long this meeting will last :/

> Ezra: Sunshine, you've got the loan. Anyone would be stupid not to approve you.

> Millicent: We'll see.

> Ezra: No seeing about it. I'll have Robert waiting at the shop to take you to the bank and from there to my place. Take a deep breath, kick ass, and take names.

The bubbles load, then disappear. I put my phone done. My assistant rearranged some meetings for me today, making it a heavier day than I'd like tomorrow. It'll be worth it. I've got a few places to drop by, things to pick up, and room to make for Millie. My phone vibrates on my desk. Seeing that it's my mom calling, I answer it. If I don't, she'll call Parker, and after his last statement of promising payback, that could mean her making a random appearance.

"Hey, Mom, feeling any better?" We touched base throughout the weekend. She did what the doctor suggested and is able to go back to work tomorrow.

"Well, hello to you, too, Ezra. Someone's in a better mood than the last time we spoke on the phone and not through text." I've got a lot of catching up to do. Messaging wouldn't have scratched the surface, plus I was around Millie all weekend, and there was no way I'd have this conversation with her around.

"I am. You still didn't answer my question, though." I put the call on speakerphone, so I can kill two birds with one stone.

"I'm much better. The doctor wouldn't make house calls. Believe me, I tried," Mom grumbles. I laugh. Her sense of humor would have Parker rolling his eyes and telling her to be quiet.

"How many times? The third time could be a charm," I offer advice before I get some of my own.

"I'm going to wait, show up back at the ER for him to take my staples out later this week. So, tell me about

Millie. I want all the details, and I have all the time in the world. It seems I'm not working today," she grumbles, always the busybody. After being cooped at up home due to her concussion, I'm sure she's ready to get back to normal.

"That's a solid idea. We see where Parker got his brains from. Millie and I are okay, or I'm trying to be. We've got some talking to do still. You know how I feel about having children. She's going to want them; there's no way Millie wouldn't. She's caring, smart, independent, a lot like a certain other woman I have in my life." I read through an email, waiting for her to respond. Boston is still in New Orleans. He's found an old historic building to use instead of one like we're in now, starting off small instead of too big, too fast.

"My other son did, too, and as far as the children, you're still young. People are having them when they're older these days. You could always change your mind, Ezra. It's not unheard of. And there's always adoption. So many children could use a man like you as a father, and from what you've said about Millie, I'm sure she'd be much the same. My boys don't pick women who don't have a heart of gold." Considering she's of the same variety, Mom is completely right.

"I don't know. I'm working through it. I've never wanted anyone the way I do Millie. She's making me rethink so much that I'm going shopping for her today." I close my computer down and stand up from my chair, putting my wallet and keys in my pocket.

"You in a store? Who are you, and what have you done to my son?" I've never liked shopping in-store for anything. Mom would shop for our clothes, bring them home, make sure we liked them, and return them if we needed a different size or didn't like them. Krista Hudson is the absolute shit, dealing with the hand she was dealt, taking on another asshole kid, and loving him like her own.

"If you'd move your ass into the city, it'd be mighty helpful right about now." Parker and I have been trying to convince her for years to move closer to us. We've offered to buy her a house, pay for all the moving fees, but she won't budge. The house she lives in now is the one both her boys grew up in, and Mom isn't ready to move.

"If Parker or you would give me something to move for, then I would."

"Your sons aren't enough? You're holding a baby over our heads to get you closer? Hmph, that sounds like blackmail." The rate Nessa and Parker go at each other, they'll have a child by the time I'm ready to get my shit together.

"I mean well. You guys are, but I'd be in the way right now. I'm not that mom who lives vicariously through her kids. Once you both are settled down, it'll be another story. Until then, I've got a doctor to chase after."

"God, that poor man has no idea what's coming for him. Love you, Mom. Don't forget to call Parker and irritate him. He's working from the house today." Maybe he'll get her to finally move out of our old neighborhood, one that no matter how much you invest in isn't being revived. Believe me, Parker and I tried. Money didn't help it, even when we bought a few houses, flipped them to help others at a decent rate. Nothing helped. We still own the houses, rent them out, but we know the return will be minimal, if not a complete loss, when Mom does decide to move.

"Oh, goodie, I'll do that. Call me if you need help shopping, honey. Love you. Bye!"

"Love you, too." I hang up the phone. I've got a lot of shit to get done and not a lot of time to do it in.

FOURTEEN

Millie

EZRA HANDLED AS MUCH AS HE COULD FOR ME, MY business plan was solid, and the outfit Vanessa walked me through via FaceTime was perfect. It was changing in the bathroom stall of the coffee shop that was hard. If I had more time, I would have gone to my house or Ezra's. Since my appointment with Perry was at four and the shop closed at three, hustling at the shop was the only option. I paired the one pair of dress slacks I own—high waisted, wide legged, dark green in color—with a white blouse. The buttons are polished gold, giving it a vintage retro feel. The mustard yellow velvet heels gave the outfit an pop of color. It was perfect in keeping myself professional while also keeping true to myself.

"Honey, I'm home," I tell Ezra as I walk out of the elevator, feeling good about the meeting after we worked through things. I can be patient; Ezra is completely worth it. He doesn't respond. I walk through the foyer, placing my bag on the big round table in the middle. The thought of work has me ready to shut down. I'm not going to pour over any paperwork tonight, or the schedule for Books and Brews. All I want is a glass of crisp white wine, dinner that's loaded with carbs, and to relax with Ezra.

"That's weird." It's quiet, and there's no response. Bill let me know Ezra was in for the night. Maybe he's in the home office. I shrug my shoulders, making my way into the kitchen. Interrupting him while in a meeting isn't on my list of fun things to do. I'm stopped in my tracks. On the kitchen counter is exactly what I need and want—a glass of wine, a bottle, a plant, and a handwritten note.

> Millicent,
> I'm so proud of you. The sky is the limit. Enjoy your glass of wine and then meet me upstairs.
> Ezra

My heart beats faster, wilder, butterflies overwhelming my stomach. The Ezra I've seen over the past few days has done a complete one-eighty. I never thought I'd see the day. It wasn't me giving him an ultimatum either, because every woman knows there is no changing a man, a red flag for sure to yourself if you thought it would ever work. So, this right here, it's another way Ezra is showing me he's working on himself for himself.

I grab the automatic wine opener, an added feature in his place since I've spent a lot of time here, the swirl of the machine working its way to take care of the cork without so much as taking the foil wrapper off. Perfect for not cutting yourself, too. I admire the plant and the fact that Ezra thought about doing something non-traditional, like a dozen roses that will eventually wilt away and die. Sure, you can press them in a book or a glass frame. This, though, means so much more, and it's long lasting, as long as you don't kill a plant, that is. Vanessa would, completely. Green thumb she is not. Black is a more apt description. My grand-mother and I used to work in her small garden every weekend. Still, when I'm over there, we find ourselves puttering in the backyard, propagating plants so I can add them to Books and Brews. My thoughts go back to the letter. I'm saving that forever, placing it in the box under my bed that holds a few other things from our time together. I grab the bottle of wine and pull the glass closer to me. A healthy pour later, and I'm heading upstairs. There's no way my anxious self could wait a second longer. The heels on my feet carry me out of the kitchen up the two sets of stairs. I notice along the way that Ezra's office door is open, not a light on, meaning he wasn't in his office to begin with. And still, I've yet to calm down in any way, shape, or form. I could recite affirmations, quotes from movies, but nothing is going to make me relax until Ezra is in my sight.

I round the corner, glass of wine in hand, having only taken a sip, and stop at the doorway. My other hand that's unoccupied reaches for the table inside the room. Ezra is sitting on the end of the bed, head dipped, elbows on his knees until he notices me. Two matching gray eyes sweep my body from head to toe. He is dressed down substantially. Gone is the immaculate three-piece suit, and in its place is a man in a cotton tee, jeans, and nothing else.

"Ezra." My eyes go to the nightstand on the side where I usually sleep, though we both land in the middle, a tangle of limbs most nights. There's a bottle of lotion that I use, a smaller plant, a book from one of my favorite authors, and my favorite lip palm.

"There's more. You've got a place in the closet and bathroom. This is only the beginning, I promise." He stands up and walks toward me. "Walk with me." He takes my wine out of my hand and places it on the table. I'd grumble if it weren't for the fact he's stunned me speechless. Where Ezra leads, I follow, first to the bathroom, where he shocks me yet again. Everything I use on a daily basis is in the shower right alongside his. A vanity drawer is much the same. And when he takes me in the closet, where there's built-ins that are amazing, I also now have a space for my clothes to hang as well as two empty drawers.

"Ezra." Tears form in my eyes. I blink them away as fast as they come, not wanting to ruin this moment.

"Don't cry, sunshine." His hand cups my neck, thumb sweeping over my jawline.

"I'm not sure it works that way." I laugh. He chuckles. The tears subside. My heart is fuller than it's ever been. Everything feels like it's falling into place, and while I was reluctant to let Ezra help me, when I finally let him in and he let me see the depth of him, it was only that much better.

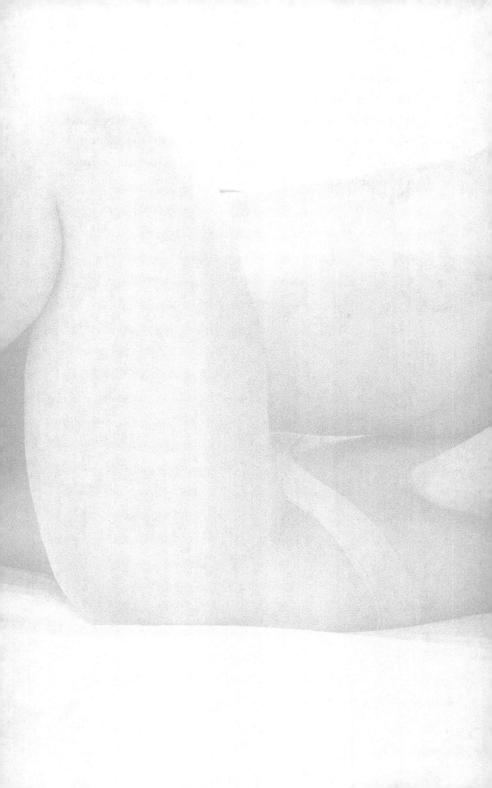

FIFTEEN

Ezra

"How'd the meeting go?" We're lying in bed, Millie's shoes kicked off, glass of wine empty, my own drink gone right along with hers. Now I've got her head in the crook of my shoulder, my fingers playing with the ends of her hair. I love that she has it down in waves. Usually, it's up in a bun, except for the early mornings or late nights.

"Really well. Perry said the business plan was perfect. He's been managing my money since the early days, has known about my idea to either buy Books and Brews or to do something even riskier and starting my own. That idea gives me hives. I mean, I've already a good rapport with all the vendors I've worked with. It would just be more of a gamble to establish my own place." Her hand slides to mine that's on my chest, tracing the vein of each fingertip before starting over again.

"Bonnie and Chad would be stupid not to take your offer and run. They don't seem to be very hands-on as it is. Plus, I know you do more than your share to a place that pays you a manager's salary when it should be double, if not more." I'm not trying to start a fight. I only want Millicent to know she's worth so much more than what they're paying her.

"That's what Perry said as well. Hopefully, by the end of the week, the loan will be approved, and then we can present it to them." There's worry in Millie's tone, one that wasn't there moments ago.

"What has you worried, sunshine?" She sits up, going to an elbow, looking at me from above. Millicent is fucking beautiful, and to think I almost lost it all. Fuck, I still could. There are a few other things I'm working through. It's not an overnight change; it can't be. Not when I've been wired like this for nearly my whole life.

"Bonnie, Chad, Scott, the espresso machine... even though it's fixed. None of them returned my calls, texts, or emails. What if they don't respond to Perry with my offer?"

"I know you don't need my help. I'm going to offer it to you anyways. It's there in whatever capacity you need." I take a breath, trying to get the lay of the land on what she's feeling. When she nods, I keep going. "Parker and I have a guy. He can do some research, figure out what's going on and go from there." Personally, I'll probably do it anyways. This has all kinds of flags waving in the air.

"It's not that I don't need or want your help, Ezra. I do, just not in a monetary sense," Millie admits.

"You think Four Brothers would be where it is today without outside help? Parker and I had to swallow our pride because we didn't bring near as much to the table. Theo and Boston had the money. We had the drive. It worked in our favor. It sucked, I won't even lie to you, feeling like you owed someone money even if those two didn't think that way at all. But, sunshine, if shit doesn't go your way with Books and Brews, you've got to start somewhere. You've got me any way you need me—money, sounding board, to paint the damn walls, I'll be here."

"Ezra, it's like you're goal today is for me to cry. I've always known there were layers to you, so many that I never thought I'd so much as get a hint of this man in front of me. Thank you." She doesn't openly accept my offer, but she doesn't shut me down either. We're making progress, which is all I can ask for. That doesn't mean I won't do something to pave her way, smooth things out as much as I can. Even if I don't tell her the truth; it's better to ask for forgiveness than permission in this case.

"You, Parker, and Krista are the only ones I've let close enough to know me, the true me. Which reminds me; Mom is coming to town soon, and I'm sure she'll use a key." A smile takes over her face, probably remembering what Nessa went through and how she thought Parker was married or had a girl-friend only to find out it was our mom.

"Noted. As if Bill wouldn't tell me otherwise. He may be your doorman, but he likes me more, Mr. Hudson."

"Is that so? It seems I may have some competition for your attention, Miss Saoirse." She's looking at me, slyness written all over her face. I take over, flipping us until she's on her back, my hips between her thighs, damning the clothes we're still wearing. I should have thought about this while we were in the closet, stripping off the layers between us, then I wouldn't have to deal with all the buttons my fingers are currently working on. Now I know how she feels when our roles are reversed.

"It seems you do. The question is, what are you going to do about it?" she teases.

"How attached are you to this shirt?" I answer her question with one of my own, ready to take us to a place where Millie is naked beneath me.

"Oh, no, you don't. This is one of my favorites, so don't you dare." Paybacks, man, they hit you when you least expect it.

"Figures. I guess I'll take my time, then," I grumble, moving so I'm sitting back, pulling my shirt over my head before taking the time to undress her, button by button, smooth skin appearing before my eyes, tits pushed up by a deep blue bra, a complete anomaly since her shirt is white, and there wasn't a hint of the color bleeding beneath it. With each one undone, more skin comes to light. My mouth waters knowing that I'll be tasting every inch of her body.

"Not too much time, I hope, please." She helps me out as I pull the end of her shirt out, leaving it lying open before I move to work on her pants. The minute I've got them open, I'm moving backwards. She lifts her legs straight up, and then they're gone, flung somewhere across the room. The lace wrapped around her chest is the same covering her pretty pussy.

"Mouth or fingers, Millie? Your choice." I give her the option, moving until I'm on my stomach, not bothering to take anything else off. I can work around any obstacle when it comes to Millicent.

"Mouth." I dip my head, smelling her sweetness, seeing her wetness seeping through her panties, knowing that I did that. My tongue licks her through the thin fabric, hands cupping the cheeks of her ass. She gets the memo and places them over my shoulders. I know she'll dig her heels into my back when I work her cunt with my mouth.

"Hands above your head. Hold on to the headboard." My eyes watch as she does what I demand. Her fingers get greedy whenever my mouth is on her pussy. They're either latching on to my hair, pressing me deeper, or she's working her nipples, and that won't do this time around.

"Ezra." My name comes out on a long sigh. My fingers move until they find the string that runs between the globes of her ass, pulling on it to add pressure against her sensitive bud.

"Fuck, look at you. Still trying to take control. Your body knows what's coming, ready for me to tongue this pretty little clit." I move her thong back and forth, watching as she squirms beneath me.

"God, do something, please. Touch me," she begs. I let the fabric go. Stretching the material out while I was playing with her works in my favor. My nose nudges it out of the way. My tongue works the whole of Millie, lapping up every delicious drop, avoiding where she needs me the most until we're both hungry for more. I thrust my tongue inside her pussy, mimicking the movement as if my cock were sliding in and out, moving my hand until my thumb works her clit the way she likes it—light at first, then harder—thighs clenching around my head, heels digging into my back. I hum, pulling my tongue out of her center, my thumb pulling on her nub as I take it in my mouth, sucking on it. "Ezra," she moans breathlessly while she comes on my face, drenching me, and this is only the beginning of our night together.

SIXTEEN

Millie

"Thanks for coming. See you next time," I tell one of my regulars, an older gentleman who comes in after the morning rush is over, staying till he's had two coffees, a croissant, and read the newspaper front to back.

"See you tomorrow, Millie." Customers like Rick are what makes me wake up each morning, excited to come to work every day. Well, there's a plethora of reasons, really—the smell of coffee brewing, the making of a different drink every time someone orders, the books that give me life on the rare occasion I get to sit down for a few minutes. It's my dream that I'm hoping becomes a reality. Another thing on my to-do list if I can make Books and Brew my own: add more food to the small variety of croissant and muffins. Maybe see if I can find a local bakery that wouldn't mind me buying off them at a discounted rate while advertising their name, a little tit for tat type of deal.

I've already talked to Nessa on my way to work, so my AirPods are put away. Ezra dropping me off here on his to the office made my morning smoother and had me in an upbeat mood, especially after last night and his multiple surprises. I grab the broom, turn the music up a smidge on the overhead speakers, listening to one of the queens of deep, raspy music singing about *summertime and the livin is easy*. If only that were true. A girl can manifest it, so that's exactly what I'll do while cleaning up the shop to save me some time later. Since Ezra made room for me at his house, I'm going to do the same. Well, maybe not buy the exact products he uses; they're not the drugstore brand, and now that my credit is being thoroughly scrutinized, I'm not using any credit cards or making crazy purchases. The shop is empty now that Rick is gone. I use the handle of the broom and do a little move of my hips while singing, figuring I've got plenty of time until a new customer comes in. Completely lost in the song, forgetting about everything, there isn't a care in my world. It's just me, the music, and my broomstick turned microphone.

"Millie, Millie, Millicent." I turn around. The only person who calls me Millicent besides my grand-mother is Ezra. Okay, I take that back. I only allow those two, and Nessa doesn't count. We both prefer to use our childhood nicknames we use with our ridicu-lous long names. At least she had an easier last name. In school, it was such a pain in the ass to have to explain to them how to say and spell not only my first but my last name as well.

"Oh, uh, I thought you were in meetings all day." I abruptly stop my dancing, wiping my now sweaty palms along my jeans, one then the other. Ezra is standing there in his suit I watched him put on today. He showed me the ropes on how to tie a Windsor knot. I almost gave up until he sat me on the counter, my thighs spread open for his body, and walked me through it again and again until I got the hang of it.

"They were rescheduled. Mom, this is my girlfriend, Millie. Millie, this is my mom, Krista." It's a good thing I know Krista is down to earth, cool as a cucumber, and loves her boys unconditionally, because this is kind of embarrassing after she watched me dance for who knows how long. Thank you, best friend of mine, for also letting me know the woman may be in her sixties but still looks like a smoke show. I make a mental note to remind myself to ask her what she does in the skin care department, because I'm not seeing a single wrinkle anywhere.

"Hi, Mrs. Hudson, it's a pleasure to meet you." I smile brightly as I walk closer to them, broom still in hand, while the other reaches out to shake hers. Never mind the fact that Ezra freaking Hudson just introduced me to his mom as his girlfriend. The man who wanted zero labels is quite literally changing his tune in every single way.

"None of that Mrs. Hudson stuff. I'm Krista. It's great to finally put a face to your name. Between

Ezra, Nessa, and Parker, I've heard about you so much that I feel like we're practically friends already." Forget shaking hands. Krista Hudson does the least of what I expect, pulling me in for a hug and holding me for a moment. My eyes are locked on Ezra. He's standing to our side, and she whispers, "Thank you for taking care of my boy." I swear the tears would come if I didn't think Ezra would lose his shit and think his mom made me cry. I nod in response instead, taking a deep breath, and then step back.

"I hope it was all good. Nessa has so much dirt on me, including pictures from our braces era, our awkward stage, and gosh, prom pictures. Though, it's two-fold. I have the same of her. As for Parker, you've raised a great man for my best friend. Ezra, though, we may have to chat." I wink at her. She chuckles, causing me to join in.

"Ha, ha. If I thought it was going to be pick on Ezra day, I wouldn't have made a sudden stop here." He pulls me closer to him, hand cupping my neck. His body dipping down, and I'm sure that my face is as red as a tomato. Which is saying something because I do not blush. That may change if he chooses to kiss me in front of his mom.

"You still would. We all know that would never stop you." And it doesn't seem to prevent Ezra from dipping his head. His lips are on mine, a lightness is surrounding us, and thankfully, there's only a teasing of his tongue sliding along my lip before he moves back.

"True. Do you have time for lunch?" he asks. It's then I notice that there's a bag on the table.

"You know the way to my heart, Ezra. Is that Eatzy's?" Nessa is obsessed with their Italian grinders, which in turn means I am as well.

"Yeah, Nessa was at the office, mentioned she was ordering it for her and Parker. Mom was there, and we decided to leave those two lovebirds alone." He makes a gagging noise, like he hasn't acted like a caveman in one form or the other.

"Oh, hush, Ezra. They've got to give me a grandbaby one of these days." I smile. My best friend will make an amazing mom. As for me, I'd like to say the same could be said. It's when that will happen is anyone's guess. Right now, I'm in my business-woman stage and that blissful-girlfriend stage as well, it would seem.

"Better Parker than me," Ezra says. Krista blows out a breath and rolls her eyes.

"I'm starving. Italian grinder?" I ask.

"Of course, with extra tomatoes," Ezra responds. We all work together to push two tables together, since they're on the smaller side and there's no way three adults could sit at one without knocking elbows, making a mess out of the place with all of the condiments.

"You're the best ever." I kiss his cheek before I sit down in my seat that he's holding for me. He does the same for his mom, showing off his ever-present manners that I know without a doubt came from Krista.

"So, tell me about yourself," Krista asks. We have lunch before the crowds come back in, and I tell her about the coffee shop, how I'm hopeful to make it my own, and all the changes I'd like. Krista adds some good ideas that I jot down in my notes on my phone to add to my boards when I get back home. I had no idea this is what I needed—hearing Ezra putting a name to our relationship, meeting his mom, and watching the two of them interact with one another. It's also clear that while Ezra may have been adopted, he's Krista's doppelgänger in the personality department.

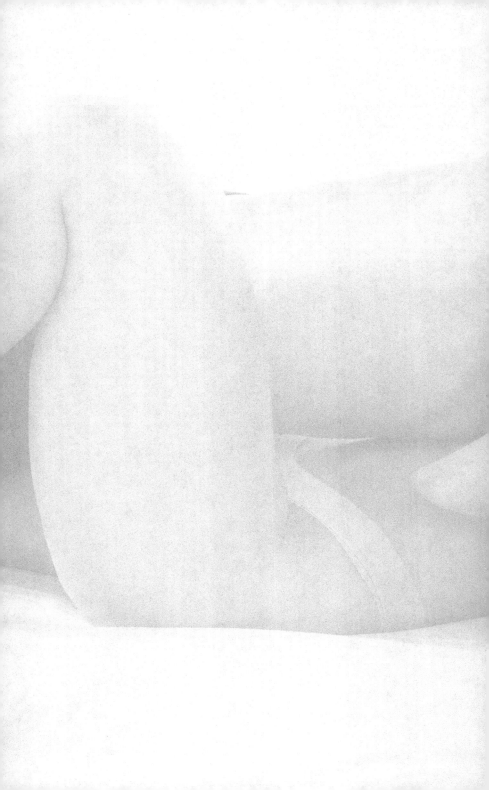

SEVENTEEN

Ezra

***

"I'VE BEEN WAITING ALL DAMN DAY TO HAVE YOU TO myself," I tell Millie once were in my bedroom, clothes off, my back to the headboard. I've got my hand on my cock, jacking it as I watch her crawl from the foot of the bed toward me, tits bouncing with each movement, hair down in a tumble of waves, and eyes heated with desire.

"And what are you going to do to me now that you have me?" The closer she gets, the more I'm itching to take control, and I would if she didn't dip her head for her tongue to meet the head of my cock, licking up the cum leaking from me. There's also the fact there's nothing better than having her ride me, and that's exactly what's going to happen tonight.

"Christ, sunshine, take my cock." My hands cup the sides of her head, allowing her to take the lead. My body, though, fuck, it has a mind of its own. My hips lift up, but since Millie is teasing me, she only takes the head, then hollows her cheeks, hands on either side of me as she holds herself steady.

"Hmm," she moans, taking another inch. The slick, velvet feel of her mouth does nothing to help hold back.

"You ready for more, Millie," I urge her. Holding back isn't happening, not now, and not fucking ever when it comes to Millicent sucking my cock. Wetness and heat surround me. A nod is all it takes for me to guide her down the length of my dick. Her eyes are watering already, the mascara she's wearing is coated beneath her eyes, and I'm not even all the way down her throat.

"Fuck, you feel good. I'm not going to come in your mouth. I want that perfect pussy of yours wrapped around my cock while you ride me," I state, hitting the back of her throat one more time. She allows me to guide her the entire time, up and then down, holding myself back from coming, knowing that her mouth works me so well, the way she tightens around me when she swallows and how she's not afraid to take my cum, sucking me dry.

When I pull her off, a popping sounds as she attempts to keep me inside. "No. Why'd you stop me?"

"Sunshine, I've waited all day to get inside you. I love your mouth, but nothing compares to your cunt. And look what arrived today." I nod toward the mirror that's leaning against the wall. The last time she rode me, back to my front, she made a comment about how hot it would be for us to see how we looked together. The fucking mirror took its sweet-as-fuck time getting here, but the view I already had while she was sucking my cock was worth it. Her ass is up in the air, back arched, giving me the perfect view of her slick wetness coating the inside of her thighs.

"How did I miss that?" She looks over her shoulder. My hands cup her tits, thumbs sliding over her nipples. There's a sharp intake of her breath when I add my pointer finger, pinching them both at the same time, a tinge of pain that she loves so much.

"We've been a little busy. You ready to watch as you fuck my cock, sunshine?"

"Ezra." Her head moves forward, eyes on mine, head dropping as she gets closer. I watch her knees, not wanting her to nail my balls, before my lips meet hers, not giving a single fuck that she was sucking my dick minutes ago. Millie has no problem kissing me after I go down on her, so why wouldn't I do the same?

"Turn around, sunshine." My hand goes to the night-stand to find a condom in the drawer. One day, I'll take her without the latex between us, but not yet. It looks as if she's going to say something; she doesn't and instead lifts a knee and places it on the outside of my hip, waiting to move the other while I work the condom onto my length. The mirror reflects how she's watching me the entire time. "You like watching my hand on my cock, Millie?" I ask once it's firmly in place, hand going to either side of her hip, guiding her.

"How couldn't I? It's hot as hell." She moves where we both need her to be. Her ass is in clear view, and I'm already planning on squeezing the globes hard enough that my handprint will be there until tomorrow.

"Nice and easy," I tell her as she lowers her body, hands on my thighs as leverage. The last thing I need is for her to take me fast and hard. The way my body is wired, I'd come entirely too fucking soon for my liking, and her not getting off first isn't happening.

"Oh God, Ezra." I watch her body in the mirror, the flush on her cheeks, the heated desire in her eyes, the way her tits are moving with every deep breath, the flare of her hips, and the way the lips of her pussy flare around the length of my cock, wetness drenching us both. A part of me is cussing myself out left and right. I could have that with no fucking barrier between the us if it weren't for my damn hangups.

"Look at you, sunshine, watch as you rise up then lower yourself down, how pretty you are taking my cock inside that tight-as-fuck cunt of yours." The tips of my fingers dig into her ass cheeks, pulling them a part to get inside of her deeper on the next downward slide. "I can tell you're close, Millie. Don't hold back. Come for me. Come all over my cock. Drench me, sunshine." Moving my hands away from her ass nearly kills me, but I don't want her to keep herself from coming. Sure, it feels good to have her cunt surrounding me, watching her fly apart. It's the best fucking visual I can ever have. I use my hands on her hips, guiding her up and down, watching the flex and pull of her muscles as we work together, as she bounces on my cock. "Work that pretty clit, Millie."

"You feel good, Ezra, so good." Her hand slides down toward her pussy, two fingers using circular motions, working herself up until she's ready. I know how Millie likes her clit played with, unhurried; it's not a race to the finish line when I'm not inside her.

"Get there. Your tight pussy is going to make me come. Take me with you, Millicent," I growl along the outer shell of her ear with each punch of my hips. Those long fingers of hers ramp things up, and it's a damn good thing, too. I wasn't joking when I said she was pulling me right along with her. The way my balls are drawing tight, it won't be long until I'm coming inside this stupid fucking condom.

"Ezra." She moves her fingers faster, up and down, side to side, head tipped back, body locking up, a throaty moan leaving her mouth, a torrent of wetness coating the two of us even more. And damn her, she's clenching down on my cock so tightly she pulls me right along with her, causing my cum to jet out of me.

"Jesus," I breathe out. Our bodies are slick with sweat, hers completely depleted of energy, falling back against my chest. There's no fucking way I'm through with her, not for a long fucking time.

"That was hot. I don't think I've ever come that hard before." I grunt, not responding. She has, multiple

times, and she'll always come like that if I have
anything do with it.

"Hop up, sunshine. I need to deal with this condom.
Plus, we both need a shower." The sheets need to be
changed, too, but that can wait until later. I've got a
craving, a craving only Millicent can quench. Our
night is just starting, and it won't end for a long time
to come.

EIGHTEEN

Millie

"Hey, Sasha, can you handle the front for a little while? I've got a call coming in," I ask when the AirPod in my ear announces that Perry from United Banking is calling. Tasha officially quit a few days ago. The girl is a basket case and had the audacity to ask for a severance package. I couldn't do anything but laugh through telling her that the only time that happens is if you were laid off. I still have no I idea how Sasha and Tasha are even remotely related.

"Not a problem," she replies, nodding. I walk—okay, fine, I *powerwalk* toward the back office, pressing on my headphone to answer the call along the way.

"Hello, this is Millie."

"Hello, Millie, this is Perry. I'm calling to follow up with you about your loan." I'm not sure if I should be excited or nervous. It's been days since our meeting and he submitted my paperwork to the loan processing department. Ezra and Perry both told me this could take up anywhere from three to seven business days, and Ezra warned me that the longer it took, the worse it might be.

"Hey, Perry, I hope this call comes with good news?" I ask with hopefulness in my voice while combatting the need to throw up what little I was able to eat this morning, since I knew it could be today or any of the next four days when I'd receive this phone call. Ezra was ready to tie me to a chair and force me to eat something before dropping me off at work. Begrudgingly, like a petulant child, I ate half a slice of toast, drank a few sips of coffee knowing caffeine on a stomach full of knots wasn't a great idea, and that was it.

"As a matter of fact, I have good news and bad news. Which would you like to hear first?" This figures. My personal life is doing freaking amazing, and my career is something I've been working on for nearly ten years, taking business classes in college and watching how-to videos in order to take my job as a barista up a notch.

"Why is that question always the hardest to answer?" I collapse in the office chair, take my hair out of its bun to assuage the tension headache that's building in my temples. I can't believe I'm admitting this to myself, but I could really use Ezra right about now. Why do I have to be this independent woman all the damn time? "Good news, please," I finally answer.

"Well, the good news is you've been approved for the full loan amount. Congratulations, Millie," Perry says.

A smile fills my face. It's going to be short-lived with bad news, I'm sure, but for right now, I'm going to take it as a massive win. There's nothing like sinking your whole life savings into a business plan that has bad news to come with it.

"You and Ezra were right," I say out loud. Perry has no idea that I'm associated with him; if I were to tack on his last name, I know I'd be treated differently, which comes with a big fat *no thanks*.

"Don't tell your gentleman friend that too much. I thank you for the compliment all the same. Now, for the not-so good news. It could be a formality, and we may not have the right address; we find that happens with snowbirds who move to Florida to retire. Sometimes, they rent a house and don't bother changing their address until they're home is built. As of right now, though, we can't contact Bonnie and Chad, Millie." That sinking feeling in my gut returns. Something isn't right. Eight months ago, we spoke weekly, then it went down to every two weeks, which was fine, no big deal. The communication slowly dwindled to once a month. These past few months, though, it's been nearly impossible to get ahold of them. Scott isn't even around, not helping at all in any situation.

"Damn."

"I know it wasn't what we were expecting. We have some feelers out. I'm hopeful to hear something soon. In the meantime, your loan is open. Try not to use your credit cards and spend wisely. If this takes longer than anticipated, we'll have to re-run your credit. And no buying a car or a home, please." He chuckles.

"Do people really do that? Don't they realize that's a huge no-no?" A car in New York city is laughable. You'd pay more in parking tickets than the car payment itself, unless you're Ezra and you're building has a garage. Even Ezra, who owns a car, doesn't drive all the time—traffic, double parking, finding a spot in itself is a pain in the ass.

"You'd be surprised. People never cease to amaze me when I come back and tell them the loan fell through. Oh, that reminds me; no sudden influxes of cash either. I know you make tips from the coffee shop. Make sure you have it written on your statements when you're making deposits." Perry told me to do that from the very beginning before I mentioned my dream of one day opening my own coffee shop.

"You got it. Well, keep me posted on if you hear anything. I appreciate everything you're doing for me." Clearly, Perry works fast—my loan, reaching out to present the offer to Bonnie and Chad, continuing to do so even though he's yet to get a response from them.

"You're welcome. I'll call you later this week regard-less. Have a good rest of your day, Millie."

"You as well, Perry." I pull my phone out of my pocket and hit the end button, unsure of who to call first. Ezra? Nessa? My grandmother? Instead of making phone calls, especially to Grandma, which would result in at least a fifteen-minute call, making me feel guiltier for leaving Tasha out there as long as I have already, I send a quick text to all three of them, then stand up, pocket my phone, and get back to work.

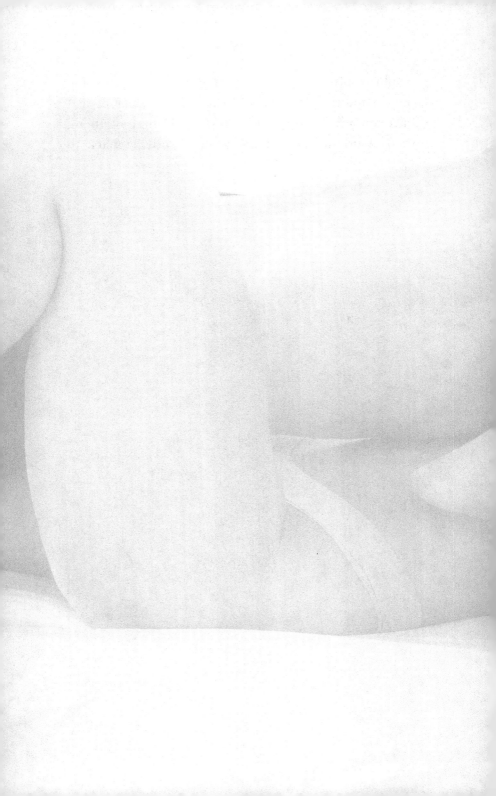

NINETEEN

Ezra
—————

THE BACK AND FORTH BETWEEN OUR PLACES IS DUMB. Yes, it was my idea. Yes, I'm kicking my own ass. No, I won't ask Millie to give up her apartment. Yet. I've still got some work to do, proving to her that I'm willing to go all fucking in.

"Honey, I'm home!" Millie's sing song voice echoes through my place. We're at my place more than hers, which is not my doing. I don't give a shit where we land as long as it's together. Millie has an obsession with my shower. Hers isn't as big, which makes it hard to join her, an activity we both thoroughly enjoy.

"I'm in the kitchen." Her text that came earlier today was a cause for celebration. I didn't have any doubt in my mind that she would get approved. The wait consumed her with so much worry, there was no amount of orgasms, mindless talking, or trash television shows that could make her shut the loan shit out of her mind.

"A girl could get used to being welcomed home this way." I'm not going to tell her my days of shopping in-store are over. One day was plenty for me to get my fill. One call to my personal assistant, and she had everything delivered by the time I got home this evening—a bottle of wine, open and at the ready, dinner in the form of sushi, salad, and the soup she enjoys so much that she finishes mine if I let it sit in front of her too long.

"That's not all there is. You've got dessert, too." Millicent isn't always big on dessert, but when she is, it's in the form of red velvet cake, cold not room temperature. Cheesecake is another—no fruit, plain and simple. In the fridge right now are both options, since I was unsure of what she would be in the mood for, if any at all.

"You spoil me." She steps up to me, hands wrapping around my neck. My hands find her hips, pulling her closer until there isn't an inch between us.

"Congratulations, sunshine. I'm proud of you." My head dips down. Our height difference is a good eight inches, making it difficult even when Millie is on the tips of her toes to kiss me. She meets me halfway. I pull her lower lip into my mouth, gaining the access I've been after all along. Her tongue peeks out, and mine twines around hers, taking over, tasting her, and dominating the kiss until her breathing becomes erratic. My hands slide until they're beneath her shirt, feeling her soft skin, thumbs sweeping beneath the cups of her bra.

"Ezra." Her fingers dig deeper into the back of my neck and shoulders.

"You make me lose my mind, Millicent," I groan against her lips, pulling away from taking things further. If we keep going, her soup will be cold, her sushi will be warm, and it'll be a total waste. Millie is a foodie. She loves any and all things related to food, not picky in the slightest, game for anything new.

"I'm not opposed to that, you know, but there is something I need to tell you, well, ask really." She steps back, grabs the glass of wine from the counter, and takes a healthy sip. I do the same with my whisky before setting it down and taking the food out of the delivery bags.

"Eat in here or on the couch? And not with you on the floor." I get that she enjoys it, but if we're going to talk, I don't want to do it with the back of her head, and my idea of fun isn't sitting my ass on a cold floor; an area rug doesn't cut it.

"Here. I'm too tired, stressed, and worried to even think about moving," she admits.

"Whoa, whoa, whoa. What's going on?" I ask as I watch her go from happy to sad. I don't let her sit in a chair; instead, I'm picking her up by the back of her thighs.

"Ezra." She lets out a squeal with a smile as I place her on the counter, wedging myself between her thighs.

"Tell me what has you on an emotional roller coaster, sunshine, and why you've held it in all day, when I'm only a phone call away." With her on the counter, our eyes meet, mine locking on hers. Even when she closes them and takes a deep before showing me those pretty green eyes of hers again.

"The loan is perfect; still on a no-spending budget. That's fine. It's not like I do a lot of that anyways. The few groceries or food I do pick up aren't enough to break the bank or put up any issues on my credit report. Perry, that's my banker, who's been with me since college, called Bonnie and Chad to present the offer to them but only got their voicemail. He also mailed a letter to their last known address. Since the phone numbers were a no-go, he isn't hopeful. That was yesterday morning. No return phone call as of yet. He said he'd keep trying. What I'm worried about the most is not being able to reach them at all. I mean, you saw what happened when the espresso machine broke down. It's been even worse lately. What if they're not answering because they don't want to sell the shop, using me until I'm all dried up after all the sweat, tears, and time I've put in?" Her shoulders slump in defeat.

"Sunshine, we've talked about this. If that's the case, which I don't think it is, we'll go from there. I'll be there helping you, no matter what. Now, you want to tell me what favor you were talking about?" Anything Millie wants, she gets, no questions asked. I'd give her fucking anything.

"Can you look into Bonnie and Chad?"

"Yep, I'll do that tomorrow," I respond right away.

"Wow. I should have known it would be easy to ask you. You're the best, Ezra. The absolute best." I kiss her forehead.

"That's all you, sunshine."

"How about we're both pretty darn spectacular," she replies as I step away, not helping her down. Millie's going to stay right where she is, and I'm going to take care of more than figuring out what's going on with the owners of Books and Brews. I'm going to feed her dinner, fuck her until she's boneless, tuck her in right beside me, and hold Millie all night long.

TWENTY

Ezra

"OH, THIS HAS TO BE GOOD," PARKER STATES AS HE walks into my office. My suit jacket is already off, and there are two to-go cups of coffee on my desk, one closer to where he's sitting down, mine near my hand. I took Millie to work, using my driver, and stayed with her while she opened, making sure everything was good to go and set up on her end. I ordered the coffee along with a kiss that I knew wasn't going to hold me over all day; I'd probably be making a trip back to Books and Brews on my lunch break. Then I made sure she locked the door behind me. Millicent is intoxicating, changing me in ways I'd have never thought possible before. Thoughts of one day asking her to marry me keep popping into my head, seeing her pregnant belly swollen with our child, a hand on her stomach as she smiles that sweet smile of hers.

"Shut up. I'd give you the whisky. Something tells me eight o'clock in the morning is too early even for you."

Getting Parker to the office last minute and without notice pissed him off, judging by the text he sent me when I asked him, long after Millie had passed out. Yet here my brother is.

"It is. So I see you've had a change of heart. Coming over to the not-so dark side, baby brother?" He's loving this.

"Something about a woman losing her shit, threatening to leave, puts life into perspective. And Jesus, Parker, you're just three months older than me. Though, you do look it too, old fucker," I respond. He knew about my aversion to labels, how I didn't feel like I'd ever bring enough to the table to make a woman feel like she was truly and deeply loved. Now, that's changing. The only thing I need to do is tell Millie how I feel, but one thing at a time first.

"We'll see who's knocking whom around in the ring this weekend and who's feeling their age," Parker responds, taking a sip of his coffee.

"Not sure who wins what. Millie has no problem fussing or taking care of me after a few of your hits." The last time, she kissed each wound, then got on her knees and gave me something else.

"Okay, that's enough of that shit. Tell me why I'm here at the ass crack of dawn when I could still be in bed with Nessa."

"She back to working nights?" That's the only reason she'd be in bed still. She and Millie have no problem getting up and moving when it's called for, especially on a trip to the market any given Saturday morning.

"Yes, it doesn't matter that we donated the bulk of the money to the new wing at her hospital. She refuses to let me play favorites and get her on days only. It's fucking with her sleep schedule and mine. My only hope is that soon, she'll be pregnant. That's the only thing that will ever slow her down," Parker admits without any kind of guilt. Unlike me, who was ready to walk away from Millie on the off-chance I was ruining her future because I didn't want a child. Mom is right. Boy, would she love to hear my inner thoughts right about now. People do change, and I am one of them.

"Well, I guess I'll tell you why I brought you in here." I take a sip of my coffee, ignoring the emails that keep pinging with a notification every two seconds.

"About fucking time."

"Millie came to me last night, asking for help. I know we don't usually use our business resources for personal matters. As you know, she's trying to buy Books and Brews. Her banker let her know yesterday that the financials were good, the loan is secure. Even if she wouldn't take my money," I grumble.

"Nessa and Millie could be sisters with the way they are about money, independent to a fault."

"Just like our mother," we say at the same time.

"Exactly. The problem is, the bank can't get ahold of Bonnie and Chad, the owners. Millie asked if I could find out where they were, worried they're ignoring her and the bank so they can keep paying her a shit wage and reaping the rewards." I tack on the last of it; those weren't her true words, but they were close enough, and it's the damn truth, too.

"So, get to work. We're not billionaires because we sat on our asses. Call our private investigator, figure out where they are, and go from there. I don't give two shits that you're mixing business with pleasure. Theo and Boston wouldn't either, which means this meeting you asked me here for was for shits and giggles. Tell me the real reason I'm here." Leave it to Parker—no holds barred, getting down to the nitty gritty.

"I want Millie to move in with me." Parker is slouched in his chair, an ankle over his knee and a shit-eating grin glued to his face.

"And? Does Millie not want to do that?" he asks.

"I haven't asked her yet." Sweat drenches my back, and it's not like Parker is Millie. I've got nothing to worry about when it comes to my brother. No judgment, only love for one another.

"Even if she says no, move her in anyways. A few phones calls, a moving company, and then she's moved in," Parker suggests.

"Now, that's an idea I haven't thought about." She'd be pissed, but it'd be worth it, and I could fuck the anger out of her.

"There you go. Thanks for the coffee. I'm going to grab a few things from my assistant, go home, and wake my woman up. I never would have thought I'd be giving out relationship advice, yet here I fucking am."

"Anytime, and thanks, Parker." My brother can be an asshole. Down to the heart of him, though, he's a good guy.

"Yep, see you later. I hear the girls are going out Saturday. Poker at your house?" Millie mentioned that she and Nessa haven't gone out in a while, so the two of them made plans to rectify that.

"That works. I'm sending them with Robert. We won't have to worry about a taxi or hired driver." Parker grumbles. I'm annoyed, too, not understanding why they can't do something at one of our places

"A man will be on them, too. No fucking way will Nessa get date raped. Damn independent woman," he adds.

"Already ahead of you. Blake has two guys lined up. I'd have preferred him, but he assured me they're the best," I tell him.

"If they're Blake's, they're guaranteed to be the best. He wouldn't have it any other way." We've known Blake for a long time. A friend we grew up with, he left and joined the Marines, got out with a plan and is now making a killing with his private security company, raking in the dough.

"True. See you Saturday," I tell his retreating back.

"See you then," he responds, then I'm left with making a call to a certain PI to get the ball rolling.

TWENTY-ONE

Millie

"DO YOU THINK THEY KNOW THAT WE KNOW?" I ASK
Nessa as we ride the elevator up to Ezra's penthouse.
We got ready in Ezra's master bedroom and bathroom, our toiletries, hair products, and dresses strewn
everywhere, only for us to pick up after ourselves once
the final product was complete. I'm in a black sheer
top, bra beneath covering everything up, black leather
pants, and pink heels. Nessa is wearing a white
bodycon dress. Neither of our men were happy that
we were going, but all the excuses in the world didn't
stop us from our night out.

"I'm pretty sure Tic and Tac called them as soon as
you gave the blond-haired one that glare of yours,"
Nessa replies.

"And you walking up to the brunette and asking for
his credentials and who hired them didn't tip them
off?" It was obvious that Ezra and Parker's names
were written all over those two security guards, which

I'm sure were paid a pretty penny; they didn't blend in at all. Plus, the fact that we were upgraded to VIP, which I knew wasn't Nessa's idea. We took one look at each other, and everything clicked into place. The driver, the free entry, so we did what any other women would do: we drank for free, danced in our area, and gossiped to our hearts' content about our men—me admitting that I love Ezra, Nessa telling me it's about time, then me pointing out that she's my favorite jerk.

We're both tipsy, holding on to one another when the doors open. Bill, who usually doesn't work late at night, must have called Ezra because there he stands, hands in his pockets, a sly grin on his face. My eyes don't move from his as I disengage from Nessa.

"Millicent." Ezra's voice is deep, eyes dark gray, desire seeping from his pores.

"Hello, Ezra," I hiccup, slapping my hand across my mouth, holding back my laughter. "I should be annoyed with you and your brother. Who hired the two buffoons?"

"Christ, remind me to fire Blake." My eyes go to Parker's and narrow.

"Parker, you realize we're not dumb. We wouldn't have gotten into any trouble," Nessa tells him.

"It's not you; it's the others. You go out without me, you've got a man on you. Especially at a fucking nightclub." Parker's tone is one that tells you, you have no leg to stand on.

"Fine, next time, a heads-up. Take me home?" Vanessa concedes rather quickly, too quickly.

"Babe, you don't even have to ask," Parker tells her. I quit looking, mainly because it's an intimate moment between the two of them. The other reason being Ezra. The tips of his fingers touch my chin, lifting it up until my eyes are on his. My best friend and her man are a distant memory. My body is on fire already.

"You have a good time, sunshine?" Ezra asks, huskily, licking his lower lip as he does. I swear a keening noise leaves my mouth without any consent from its owner.

"The best. Tic and Tac are awful buzzkills, though. It's hard to talk about the number of orgasms our men give us when they're listening in the corner." The cinnamon-flavored shots Nessa and I ordered have seriously lowered my inhibitions in the form of my mouth running like the roadrunner.

"And how many orgasms did I give you in one night?" Ezra asks. I use my fingers, counting that one night he literally wrung my body dry, using his mouth twice, then his fingers once, and his cock at least once before I passed out, only for him to wake me up an hour later with his cock sliding in and out of me again.

"Five?" It's more of a question than a statement, unsure if the number is actually correct or not. That night was a lot of firsts. Ezra gave me more than his body; he gave me his emotions as well.

"Then tonight, we'll go for six. Are you going to remember tonight come the morning?" His hand cups my neck, thumb on my jaw in his signature move when he's within reaching distance of me.

"Ezra, any night that ends with you, I will never forget." I may be a little tipsy, nothing that would ever make me not remember a moment with him.

"That's good. I'm going to take my time with you tonight, Millicent. I've been without you for nearly four hours, stuck playing poker with Parker, who's a piss-poor sport, making Theo leave early with all of our money. And now I'm going to make up for a night we could have spent alone all along." A shiver races down my spine. He's right. We could have had another evening alone, one that we both would thoroughly enjoy. I needed a night with Nessa, though, like she needed one with me. While we got ready, it was like we were back in college, ready to hit the bar scene, drinking and carefree. So, tonight was one of those where we could push our worries away, me more than Nessa, have some fun, talk, dance, and come home to our men.

"I'm sorry. Kind of. I'll make it up to you."

"Damn right you will." His mouth slams down on mine, taking it with his. He walks until my back meets the nearest wall. I can feel his heaviness between my thighs, which tells me tonight is going to be one where we both give and take. And it's going to start with me on my knees as soon as our kiss ends.

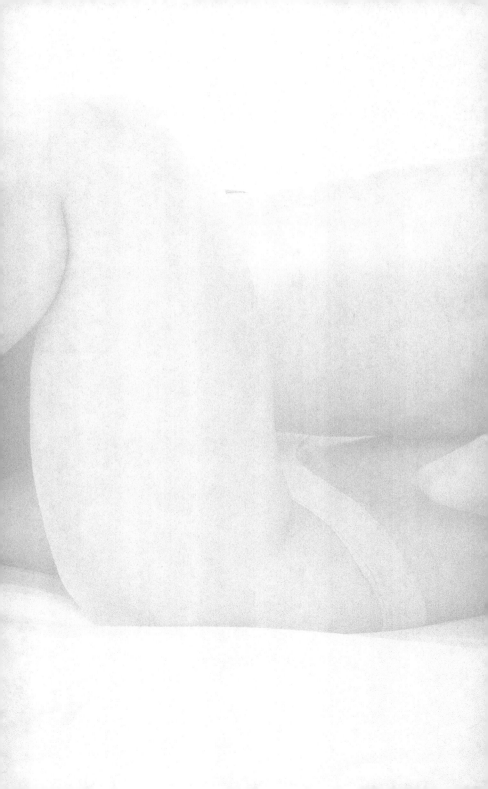

TWENTY-TWO

Ezra

___

SHOES GONE, CLOTHES GONE, BOTH OF US COMPLETELY bare. The minute we made it through the bedroom door, she was stripping, and I was following her lead. Millie isn't drunk; she's tipsy as fuck. And what I have to tell her, I'm praying like fuck she's going to remember come morning. "Millicent," I get her attention as she checks me out the lazy way from head to toe before her eyes land on my cock that's pressed along my abdomen,

"Hmm," she responds, licking her lips. No Goddamn way is her mouth getting anywhere near my dick, not tonight.

"I'm taking you tonight. No condom, no pulling out. I'm coming inside you for the first time ever, sunshine. I'm giving you a piece of me I've never allowed anyone to have." I'm not bringing names into the bedroom, nor my past. Nothing but the truth she needs to know. How deeply I feel for her, it's forever. I'm never going to let her go.

"Ezra, are you sure?" She sits up faster than I thought possible with how she was laid out in front of me, thighs spread wide open, one hand cupping her tit, pulling on her nipple, the other slowly skating a path down the center of her abdomen, so close to her plump lips, giving me a show I'd usually have to guide her with if it weren't for the alcohol she has in her system.

"I've never been more sure Millie. You deserve this, I deserve this, we fucking deserve this. I don't want any more barriers between us, physical or emotional," I admit as I take a step closer to her body. She's fucking gorgeous, brings you to your knees. Her soul is nothing but beautiful. For the longest time, I didn't think anyone would take me as I am, that I was undeserving of unconditional love. Krista and Parker may have given it to me when I was younger, but as an adult, it's the woman before me who proved it to me every step of the way.

"Oh, Ezra, this gift, I'll cherish it forever. I promise you that I'm yours. You can always trust me, okay?" Fuck, this woman owns me.

"Okay." There's a tremble in my voice. Shit, there's probably one in my whole damn body. This step is huge, it's permanent, and it's one that settles in my soul.

Millicent's hand reaches out for mine, locking our fingers together, spurring me to move. Her back flattens on the mattress, my hips settling between her spread thighs. My cock is ready to slide deep inside her after that one time where just the fucking tip was being swallowed by her tight pussy. I swore I'd do anything to get to where we are now. It was heaven and hell. Heaven because it felt so fucking good and hell for having to leave the clutch of her center.

My mouth touches hers, sucking her bottom lip, nipping at it before letting it go. Her tongue slides out to search for mine, so I abandon her lips to give her what she wants while my hands cup the sides of her neck, taking as much as she's giving. I'm greedy for her. Never have I ever felt this emotion. I deepen the kiss, trying to convey my thoughts without saying the words.

"Ezra," she moans. My cock is brushing the lips of her pussy with every moment it strokes along her clit, wetting the underside of my length.

"You ready for this, sunshine? I can't guarantee how long I'll last, but you can't hold back." Christ, I feel like a damn virgin, ready to nut the second you get inside someone.

"The way you're teasing me, I won't last long either." Her own voice is choppy, breathless in a way. I pull my hips back, grunting at the loss of her heat searing me from the outside in.

"We'll come together." A shudder leaves me when the head of my cock glides inside, wetness helping along the way. The feeling is out of this world. "Sunshine, you can't do that," I tell her when her pussy flutters along my length, baring down in a way that makes me stutter step.

"I can't help it. It feels… wow." That's one way to put it. Another inch, another deep breath, one after another until I'm planted completely inside of Millie. My head drops between her breasts. Keeping my cool is a thing of the past.

"It feels more than wow. Jesus, I could have had this with you all along. I can feel everything. Your wetness, the soft satiny feel of you clutching my cock. Son of a bitch, Millicent, I will never use a condom with you ever again." I lift my head. Her green eyes meet my gray ones. It's then that I realize this isn't just sex. It's more than that. I slowly pull my hips back and slide back in.

"Ditto, but, well, you know, maybe a bit different. Oh God, that right there." I roll my hips, watching as her eyes glaze over with a different type of desire. It's a need unlike before, and thank you, God, she's on the same page. I move until my forearms are on either side of her head, caging us in, watching her the entire time. She closes her eyes when I swivel my hips as I thrust inside of her tightness. She sighs in pleasure, the yearning need when I pull back only to glide inside.

"Millie, eyes open," I groan. That ripple is her tell. She's about to come, and I want to watch.

"Ezra." She does as I ask.

"I want your eyes on me when you come, taking me with you." Her gaze stays locked on mine. The rasp of her nipples along my chest, the way her legs are wrapped around my waist, locking tighter than they were, heels pressing deeper, it all pushes me closer to the edge.

"Ezra." My name leaves her lips when she comes around my bare length, sucking the come out of me with every clench. Fuck, the feeling, it's indescribable. I'll never forget this moment. Ever.

TWENTY-THREE

Millie
———

"Wake up, sunshine." I swat at Ezra's head whispering into my ear at some ungodly hour, I'm sure. Last night, he had no problem claiming my body, giving me multiple orgasms, barely taking a nap in between until one of our hands was finding the other.

"It's too early. Go away," I grumble into the mattress. My head is somehow under the pillow. Ezra lifted it up, so light is pouring through the small gap, which means it's later than I usually sleep in on a Sunday morning. The one day a week when I've got zero responsibilities in the adulting department except for grocery shopping and cleaning. Given that most of my time is spent at Ezra's, even that isn't much to do.

"Millicent, it's close to noon. You sleep all day, what are you going to do tonight?" He moves until he's lying behind me, hand sliding up my side. I'm on my stomach, naked from last night, preferring to not put anything on after our last orgasm. I knew there was a chance he'd just rip it off of me. A woman can only buy so many pieces of clothing before she gets tired of replacing the items.

"What?" I roll over until we're face to face, blinking the sleep away. Ezra's completely dressed, and not in lounge clothes. He's in a white cotton shirt and jeans. I love dressed-down Ezra on a Sunday morning, and I'm missing it, damn it all to hell. "I'm getting up. I need a shower, to brush my teeth, and coffee."

"That can wait. The private investigator reached out to me this morning. The reason why I'm dressed and not in bed with you is because of that call. Sunshine, you wore me the fuck out." Ezra is only eight years older than me. Forty is not old by any stretch of the imagination, but being told you wore your man out, it's pretty freaking spectacular.

"Me, little ole me wore out Ezra Hudson. I find that hard to believe since it was you who wanted to beat your personal record in the orgasm department," I tease him. I love seeing that gleam of pure male pride in his eye. "Should I get dressed for the first half of the conversation regarding what your PI told you?"

"It might not hurt. Everything is on my computer. Don't take too long, okay?" He places a kiss on my nose before he rolls away and climbs out of the bed. I watch as the corded muscles in his back ripple beneath his shirt, even with the worry settling back in my stomach, a worry that was gone for a few short days when Ezra told me he'd step in and help. It has now returned with a vengeance. Add in the lack of food and the fact I'm still waking up, and I'm liable to lose whatever is in my body from our early dinner before going out.

"I won't." I flop onto my back, arms going outwards, and take a deep breath, holding it in before letting it out.

"Millie, sunshine. It's not horrible. We'll get through this," he reassures me as he walks out of the bedroom. I take another breath then sit up. The sheet slides off my body, the air conditioning causing me to shiver now that the covers are gone.

"I'm getting up. Jeez." What a way to wake up. Maybe I should rethink this owning and operating a business. So far, all it has been is a pile of stress. I grab the shirt Ezra was wearing yesterday and pull it over my head while sitting on the side of the bed, doing this awkward dance while my legs are crossed. If Ezra were to see me now, there's no doubt in my mind we'd both forget about what his private investigator found out.

"Coffee is brewing!" he calls out while on the stairs, or what I'm assuming are the stairs with the way his voice echoes. I'm out of the bed, stomping to the bathroom to handle my morning business before washing my hands and brushing my teeth. The show I'm craving will have to wait until afterwards. It's Sunday, which means it's time for the weekly task of exfoliating, shaving, washing my hair, and applying a face mask of some kind. I take my self-care serious on the one day a week I don't have to get to the shop. All the other days, I'm up and at Books and Brew by six thirty in the morning in order to open our doors at seven. I'm still cold when I walk out of the bathroom minutes later. The closet has what I need. A few changes of clothes of mine hang alongside Ezra's, but that's not what I'm after. I locate a hoodie that will drop to mid-thigh right along with his shirt I'm wearing and a pair of slippers that are two sizes too big on my feet.

Unable to prolong the process any longer, I shuffle my feet out of the bedroom, then down the stairs as the sun shines brightly in every direction. I kind of wish it were dark and gloomy, a mood that is sure to match the news I'm about to receive.

"Don't you look cozy?" Ezra meets me at the door to his office with two cups of coffee in his hands. You'd think I would be a snob about the dark goodness. I'm not, especially if I don't have to make it.

"I didn't feel like getting dressed when I'd just be changing again to take a shower. Thank you." I take the steaming hot cup out of his hand, closing my eyes as I take the first sip.

"Alright, come on. I'll make us lunch after this shit is out of the way." His free hand goes to my lower back, leading me until we're inside his office and he's sitting behind the desk, not letting me go until I'm sitting in his lap.

"One more sip, then I'll be coherent enough," I tell him, placating myself more than him.

"You're already wide awake. Our PI, Blake, went down to Florida to scope out the last known address on Bonnie and Chad," Ezra dives right in. I place my cup of coffee on his desk. The gleaming wood is beautiful. I find a scrap piece of paper, lift my mug, and then put it down so it doesn't leave a ring.

"Okay." I look at the computer, reading the places Blake went. One town led to another, which is what Perry expected. What I didn't see coming was the fact that they took a plane home six months ago, one-way, and that's when the trail went cold. "Am I reading that correctly? They're here in New York yet ignoring every call or message? Ezra, what the hell is going on?" My questions tumble out, one after the other. Nothing is making a lick of sense.

"You are. Blake found a couple of other things. Their house here is vacant. He sat on it once he figured out they left Florida. He's going to present it to the cops, let them know what's been going on and let them take it from there," he finishes. It's been maybe three days, if that, and this Blake guy was able to do all this. Jesus, money really does talk.

"Okay, should I keep the coffee shop open? I'm not sure what the right thing to do is. Are they missing? Did they have an accident? Did they just pick up and leave? That would be hard to believe. They trained me, knew that I wanted to potentially buy Books and Brews from them. Something isn't right, Ezra. Something really isn't right." I drop my arms to the desk and rest my head on top of them, doing some deep breathing because this stinks, stinks to high freaking heaven.

"Continue on as planned until we're told anything differently. If you don't mind, I'll call Perry and fill him in about the situation, send him as well as the detective who will be handling the case the contact information. No sense in your loan sitting open until we know something." One of his hands moves to my back, rubbing it in gentle circles.

"Yep, that's fine. I'm just going to have a pity party for one over here. Why does this shit have to happen to me? And now I feel guilty. What about Bonnie and Chad? Oh, Jesus, what about Scott?" I sit back up, moving so I can see Ezra's face.

"Breathe, sunshine. Let's see what happens and where to go from there. It's your day off. Try to focus on that girl stuff you always do. I'll make lunch, and we'll go from there, okay?" He calms me down.

"Okay, right, you're right." I take a deep breath. He moves me until I'm settled more comfortably in his lap, wrapping his arms around my body and comforting me in a way only he does.

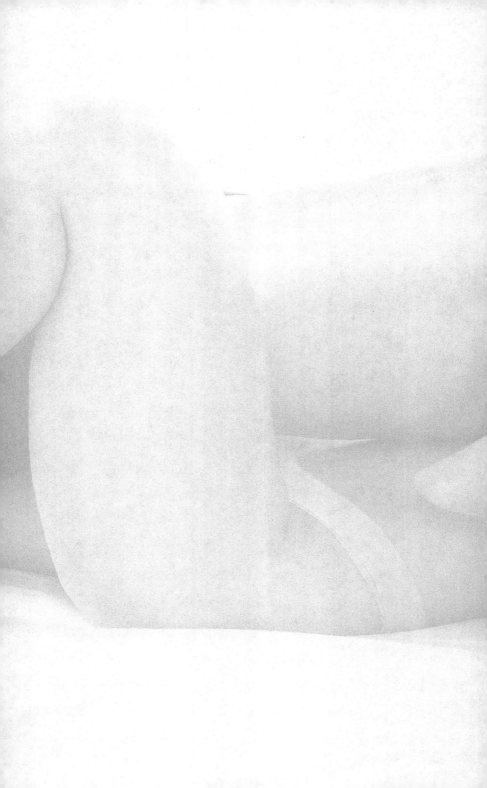

TWENTY-FOUR

Ezra

"ARE YOU FEELING BETTER?" I ASK MILLIE AFTER what seems like hours later. She's been holed up in the master bathroom since she calmed down from the news I handed her. I kept myself busy, emailing Blake back, calling Parker to let him know in case Millicent calls Nessa and needs her in a way only a woman can console her, by talking their ear off for hours and hours on end about the same thing. It's what they need, and while she knows I'm there for her no matter what, the comfort Millie needs is her best friend.

"Kind of. Thank you for handling all of this for me. I'd have already given up," she admits. An over-sized tee shirt, one of her own, covers her body. She's got leggings on beneath them, hair down in curls from it air drying, skin that pinkish color where it's not covered up.

"It's not in your nature to give up. You would have figured something out or kept pushing through. It's who you are, Millicent." A quality I love about her. I had that epiphany long before right now, that she's it for me. It took a lot of fucking soul searching and talking to my mother, and I'm talking daily, with her listening to my worries, telling me that I'm making up excuse after excuse. I've broken the cycle already, never having touched a drug in my life.

"I'm not so sure about that in this equation." Millie plops down on the couch. Sandwiches, chips, cookies, and drinks are on the coffee table in front of us. I pull it closer so she won't sit down on the floor even though it's what she prefers. The temperature outside has dropped, and even with the heater running, it's still too cold to sit on a damn floor.

"Millicent, I'm not going anywhere, not now or ever. I was going to wait to tell you this after the news I delivered this morning, but I'm tired of fucking waiting. We've done that enough due to my stupidity." She is looking at me, nothing but the pure sunshine that she is. The world weighing heavily on her chest, yet she's pushing through. Not allowing it to pull her down. "What you need to know is that my future is right in front of me. I want you any way I can have you." She crawls her way toward me, hands going to my cheeks, legs straddling my lap.

"Ezra." Only she can say my name like she does—soft, sweet, and breathless.

"Sunshine, I love you. Took me almost losing you to pull my head out of my ass and do a shit ton of soul searching. I'm not letting another day go by that you don't know what you mean to me. I want everything. I want you to move in with me, and soon, my ring on your finger, and one day, our child growing inside you, if that's something you want. The last part, that is. You're moving in and marrying me no matter what." I wipe away the tears that slide down her cheeks, memorizing this moment. Even if Millie doesn't reciprocate the words, this is enough. It will always be enough as long as she's around.

"I love you, Ezra." A breath I didn't know I was holding leaves me, proving to me once again that I don't always know what's best, even for myself. "And I'll move in with you. Not right away, though. I'm still in a lease, and with all that's going on, I'm pretty sure Perry would have a coronary if I changed addresses in the midst of everything else. As for a child, I'd be honored to have a child who looks like you, has the drive that you do, loves so deeply, but I can wait. And I'd like to wait, too. I'm still young, and you're not, *ahem*, that old," she jokes about my age. I ignore the barb because I am not fucking old.

"I want to make Books and Brews or whatever comes my way a smashing success, have time to enjoy it being the two of us before we bring a child into the equation." My mouth takes hers. I like what I'm hearing, the determination to get through another obstacle thrown her way. I move us until she's flat on her back, my elbows on either side of her head as I show Millicent what her words mean and do for me. The bad start of the day is turning into a late afternoon that's better than expected, and when Millie wraps her legs around me, my cock comes to life beneath my jeans as I drag it along the seam of her pussy.

"Are you too sore for this, sunshine?" I ask, pulling away. Her hair is wild, lips plump, cheeks flush when I drag my mouth away from hers and look at her.

"Would you hate me if I said yes?" That doesn't stop her from tightening her hold on my hips. My woman doesn't want me to leave, and I'm not mad about that.

"Nope. You took me hard last night." It was fucking heaven on earth. "We'll eat, watch some TV, then I'll use my mouth."

"Okay, maybe I'll return the favor." She winks at me. I dip my head down again, lips grazing hers, getting one more taste of the woman I love.

TWENTY-FIVE

Millie

"I'LL BE RIGHT THERE!" I HEAR THE CHIME TO THE door of the shop while I'm in the bookstore part, shelving a few new books that were brought in, as well as tidying up. My weekend was full of ups and downs, more ups than downs, which made it easier to get out of bed this morning, pretending like there's nothing wrong, everything's fine, everything's okay, right?

"Hey, sunshine." I turn around from my spot, where I was shoving a book into an empty spot, confused as to why Ezra is here. He's taken so much time off and away from work, not that he told me. I knew it because, well, frankly, he's been with me more than usual. It was why I told him I'd meet him at his place tonight and shooed him off when he tried to stay longer than normal after dropping me off today.

"Ezra." My face must show my confusion. It's a few minutes before closing, and I'm honestly ready to go back to his place and collapse on the couch. Putting on a brave face when your job could potentially be taken away isn't for the faint of heart.

"I'm here with my attorney. The detective leading the investigation has a few questions. I've locked the door already, and my lawyer is currently pulling the shades down. You're not in trouble. Sylvester is here as a precaution. You look at him if you feel uncomfortable answering. If you don't, he'll take it from there. Blake gave me the heads-up. I was able to meet him with the detective." I'm pretty sure my heart is beating out of my chest. I've never had an incident before that warranted a police officer being in my presence, let alone being questioned.

"Okay." My palms are sweaty. Hell, my whole body could be. I wipe them down my jeans then take my hair out of its bun, trying to appear more professional and not like the haggard train wreck I'm sure I look like after working all day without help. Tasha had class all day, which meant our busiest day was down to only one barista, my down time nonexistent.

"You're not in trouble. We shouldn't keep them waiting just the same." Ezra head dips down, hand going to my neck, fingers massaging what they can, and plants a small soft kiss on my lips.

"You're right." I pull away, squaring my shoulders, and head toward the unknown, what no woman wants.

"Sylvester Sterling, Detective Johnson, this is Millie." I shake both of their hands. Sylvester is definitely in a league of his own. His three-piece suit looks much like Ezra's, meaning it costs thousands upon thousands. Detective Johnson is in a standard button-down shirt and slacks, badge on his hip.

"It's nice meet you, Mr. Sterling and Detective Johnson. I'm sorry. We'll have to pull some tables together if you'd like to take a seat," I offer.

"That won't be necessary. As you know from Mr. Hudson, Blake handed off what he found. I need to know when your last phone conversation, text, and email communication you've had with Bonnie and Chad Smithers took place," he dives right into the questions.

"Phone calls, I'm not sure. Probably months, which is weird. They used to check in a lot more. I figured they were enjoying their retirement. The last email I received was nearly a month or two ago. About the same time Scott quit coming in to check the books. It wasn't until the espresso machine went down and I tried to reach any of them that I really started paying attention to how little communication there had been. Then again, Scott was here to glance over things and then left as fast as he came. It was when I wanted to present an offer that I knew something wasn't right when Perry, my banker, couldn't find them. That's when I asked Ezra to step in." I quit talking because I've blathered on more than what Detective Johnson asked. My nerves cause me to talk more than I usually would.

"Is there a way you can go back in your emails and print those off as well as jog your memory as to when Scott was here?" I look at Mr. Sterling, not because I'm guilty, not in the least; I just don't know where to go from there, if that's legal without a warrant. See what I mean? I know freaking nothing.

"You can give them to him. It'll make thing easier than getting a subpoena," Sterling answers my unanswered question.

"Right, well, the work computer is in the back. That's the only way I communicate with them, and the work line. I can pull the security feeds, too, as far as when Scott has come in. As for texts, the last ones I sent were on a whim, and they never responded, but you can have those as well."

"We'll start with the emails. We've filed a missing person's report on Mr. and Mrs. Smithers." A gasp escapes me. I'm lost for words. The two people who entrusted me to take care of their shop are missing. It shouldn't shock me, yet it does. Damn it, I should have brought this to Ezra's attention way before now.

"Okay, give me a few minutes, and I'll go print them off." I see the look on Detective Johnson's face. He doesn't want me to leave his sight. I look at Ezra, confused. Surely, this guy doesn't think I've done something to them. I'm no criminal, and taking out a loan and asking your boyfriend to look into things and he hires a private investigator don't scream person of interest. A criminal would keep the deposits and set up shop like it was theirs, which is not what I did.

Nope, I took on all the responsibilities while staying true when doing payroll, too.

"Sterling and Johnson will go with you, Millie," Ezra states, not leaving it up for interpretation any longer. It's probably killing him that he didn't suggest that he would go back there with us.

"Yes, lead the way, Miss Saoirse," Ezra's attorney states. Well, he's technically mine as well, I guess. I can't even think about the hourly rate he's charging Ezra, adding on to what I already owe him. It'll be an argument about when or if I can pay him back, which he'll never accept, meaning I'll have to get creative.

"Of course." I walk away, feeling their presence behind me as we walk. The office will for sure feel even smaller than it already is with two big-bodied men in there with me. A few steps around the counter, an opening of a door, the light turning on automatically, and we're in the office. I wake the computer up with the mouse, go to my work email, and pull all our conversations up.

"How far would you like me to go back?" I ask Detective Johnson. They left early last summer for their retirement to Florida, so it's been about eight months since I've seen them in person.

"As far back as you can. I'd like to get a clear timeline," Johnson replies. I'd make small dick comments in my head with a last name like Johnson if he were rude. His demeanor isn't; he's short and to the point, probably thinking this isn't worth his time but having to deal with it since Ezra's name is involved.

"Okay." I click through our thread, selecting all, and then click print. The papers come out. Thank God for a laser-jet printer. There's no warming up, running out of ink constantly. The sooner it's done, the faster we're out of this small room.

"One more question about Scott. Have you noticed if his behavior was more unusual than normal?"

"Umm, Scott wasn't really the talking type. He'd say hi, look at the deposits, withdrawals for inventory or services, then the schedules, and after that, it was a quick goodbye. Honestly, he was never here for more than twenty minutes. I left him to it usually, because Scott came when it was our busiest time and I had to handle the front either by myself or with the other barista who works here." I'm once again word vomiting like it's my job.

"Thank you. If you have any further questions or can think of anything else, your attorney has my card. Please don't hesitate to use it." We shake hands. I'm grateful the questioning was over as fast as it was.

"You did good. Let's get back out to Ezra before he has my damn head," Sylvester jokes. I nod, still in shock about today's events, following in his tracks, only looking up when Ezra meets us behind the counter. My arms wrap around his body, and I take what feels like a deep breath.

"If you need anything else, you have my number. I'm taking her home. Thanks again, Sly." I've tuned the rest of the conversation out, too numb to think about anything else. As long as I'm in Ezra's arms, I know I'm safe and protected, and that's all I need.

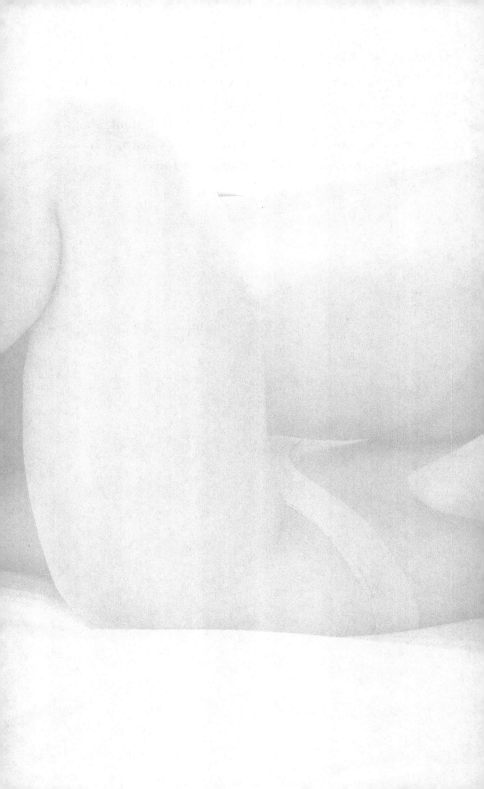

TWENTY-SIX

Ezra

"SO, ANYBODY HAVE ANY INSIGHT ON HOW WE CAN move this along?" Blake, Sly, Parker, Theo, and Boston are sitting in front of me, trying to form a game plan. It's been two days since Detective Dickhead started his investigation. It didn't matter that Blake handed over everything he had on the Smithers, which was on the up and up. It was Scotty boy who was a big concern, not that they'll take Blake's word for it, so we kept that information to ourselves. The problem is, after forty-eight hours of Millicent worrying, biting her nails, tossing and turning at night, I'm tired of not stepping in. If there's something I can do to move things along, I'm more than open to it.

"I can send it anonymously to a news channel. It might create a stir for Millie, though. Is that something she'd be able to handle? Whatever happens, it's going to garner attention regardless," Blake states.

"Better you than me. It means the shop will get media, you'll get media, and so will Millie. Think about that before you pull the trigger," Parker inserts.

"Fuck, if it were just me, I wouldn't care. You know Millie; she's like Nessa. Neither of them care about our money or the fame that comes with Four Brothers." I run my hand down my face. We're all in the conference room at our office building. The glass windows are smoked out, so no one can see what or who we're talking with.

"If we time things right, you let out what you know about Scotty to the media. I can make a statement about myself leaving New York, leaving dear old dad in the background. It would still shed some light on what Scott has been doing, forcing the police department's hand while also putting it out there that the only son of Governor Wescott is leaving the fold even more." Boston willing to throw himself out there onto the chopping block is not what I expected.

"Boston, there's no coming back. You're as good as written off. You do this publicly, without letting him know first, is that something you can deal with?" Theo asks, taking the words right out of all our mouths, especially Parker's and mine. We're the two from the wrong side of the tracks. New money. And Wescott makes sure we know it on the rare occurrence we've had to be in his presence.

"Yep. Talk to the lawyer and PI. I'm out of here. Need to wrap a few things up. I hope it all works out for your girl. This fucking state is too damn cold, and if I don't do this my way, he'll spin it in a way that'll make it ten times worse." Boston stands up, nodding in a way that tells us he'll talk to us about his plan later.

"Alright, I'm with Boston on this. Once the dust settles, buy the fucking building under our shell name. Millie will never be the wiser. The Smithers are renting. It'll be business as usual once the media frenzy calms down," Theo suggests.

"Not a bad idea. Does Vanessa know about our shell company?" I peg Parker with a stare. He tells her everything, and it will fuck me over if he has.

"No, she doesn't, cocksucker. So, do what needs to be done. Sly is here. Have him make an offer the owners can't resist. Make the transition easy on everyone." Sly has been quiet the majority of the time, watching how things unfold. The bulldog sits and waits for the perfect opportunity to attack.

"I already have an offer drawn up. This was going to be my suggestion regardless. It's a prime piece of real estate; you can control the rent while still recouping the cost of purchase. I'll handle all the paperwork, in case something should come up, which is doubtful. It's under the shell corporation, and I'm the one handling everything," Sly states. It's a plan that would work for everyone. The reason for the business loan was to purchase everything from the Smithers. With what Blake has alluded to, Bonnie and Chad won't be able to sell anything, Scotty boy will more than likely be behind bars for the foreseeable future, and with the shell corporation being the building holder, it would be easier.

"Ezra, you're going to have to give her the news gently. As much as the past six months have been hard on Millie with doing everything, the girl has a bleeding heart. She loved the two of them, will more than likely try to shoulder the blame for not putting two and two together sooner." Fuck me running. Parker isn't wrong. Millicent wears her heart on her sleeve, so this is going to wreck her world.

"I'm going to send this to the owner. If you'll excuse me." Sly stands up, grabs his bag, and we shake hands, my mind still on how to break the news to Millie. If I should tell her tonight or let her watch it on the news. I think hearing it from me will be the best plan of action.

"Ezra, Parker, my invoice will be sent to you. I'll see myself out. A pleasure like always." Blake takes his leave.

"And then there were two, huh?" Theo left after Boston, who had a meeting on the west coast coming up and still had to talk to his assistant. My suspicions are that Boston wanted more than paperwork from her, is more like it.

"Seems to always be. Is Nessa working tonight?" Assuming I tell her once we're both home for the evening, I'll be there to hold Millie while she lets it out, but she'll no doubt be calling Nessa and her grandmother. Maybe I'll call Mom, have her come down this weekend. She, Millie, and Nessa can do whatever it is that girls do—shop, gossip, sit around and bitch about the men in their lives.

"She isn't. I'll make sure we don't have any plans. If we do, I'll reschedule them. Is Mom still after the doctor who stapled her?"

"Thanks, and no. Said something about when she got her staples out, that he wasn't as handsome as she remembered. I'm thinking she lied about how bad her concussion was. Mom also said the only reason she'd even think about moving is if one of us had kids, so pony up, brother. Millicent and I aren't there yet. In fact, it might be another couple of years before we are." It means we'll have more time to practice, and I'm okay with that.

"About Goddamn time. Don't worry. We're not *not* trying." Parker pauses, a smile taking over his face. "Good luck tonight, brother. Keep me posted. I'm here if you need me. Well, not in the office, because fuck that. I still have no idea why you choose to work in a stuffy building, but to each their own." Parker hates dealing with people on a daily basis unless it's Vanessa or family. Everyone else can fuck off for all he cares. I'm the opposite, thriving on the noises, the chaos. Sitting at home working in the quiet usually has me doing the opposite of working.

"Thanks, I'm going to need it."

TWENTY-SEVEN

Millie

"Oh shit, I know something is wrong if you're meeting me at the door and not in the kitchen." It's already unusual for Ezra to beat me back to his place when I get off work a lot earlier than he does. Ever since we admitted our feelings to one another and he told me he wants me to move in with him, I've spent my nights here. I still have to figure out if breaking my lease, let alone moving, would mess up my loan. That will have to wait until tomorrow. The look on Ezra's face is anything but happy. A forlorn look is securely in its place. "What happened now?" I drop my backpack to the ground and step out of my sneakers, tired of my feet being caged in from being on my feet all day. I'm really going to have to look at a new pair of sneakers or hire actual help.

"Come on, sunshine. You're going to need to sit down for this." Ezra dips his head and kisses me lightly before he pulls away, his hand going to mine.

"I can't take any more bad news." I dig my heels in when he tries to get me to move, literally. My mind has been plagued by what-ifs, feeling like I'm in some kind of horrible dream. The only light at the end of the tunnel is Ezra, and should he give me any bad news about our relationship, I will literally curl up into a ball and rock in a corner.

"That look, get it out of your head now. Nothing is wrong with us. We are rock fucking solid. We're not ever going down that path again. We're in this forever. I get you're going to have doubts. I put those there, and I'll work my hardest to erase that shit. This is about something else entirely, okay?" I look at his face, really see him. My shit is affecting him. The way I've been in my own freaking head, worrying about myself and basically blocking off the entire world. I haven't even called my grandma or Vanessa. I'm a total shit head. I'll have to do that after Ezra and I talk.

"I know we are. I just had a moment. The way you met me at the door, telling me we have to talk. It does things to a woman who's so in love with the man in front of her that it aches to even think about no longer having you in my life. Thank you, Ezra. You've done so much, have showed me nothing but an abundance of patience, and I'm sorry for doubting us." This has been one hell of a day, week, month— months really—that it's all starting to bleed together.

"You've got nothing to be sorry about. I really do need to let you know about something before it's broadcasted on the news, though, okay?" He clasps the side of my neck, our eyes locked on one another.

"Okay, but on a scale of bad news, is this a one glass of wine or the whole bottle?" Ezra's hand slides from its place on the side of my face down to my shoulder, squeezing it in a way to bring me comfort before moving down the length of my arm until he reaches my hand, taking it in his, and then were walking further into the house. I take a deep breath, preparing for the worst but hoping for the best. My mind is going in every which direction while my eyes are gazing around the whole of Ezra's place. Vanessa was right. These brothers are a lot alike, especially in the decorating department. The basics are laid down— the furniture, area rugs, the necessities. But there's not a whole lot in the way of color or decorations, not even in a throw pillow on his couch. My plant is literally the only thing that isn't the shade white, beige, or black. When I move in, my things will mingle with his, co-existing together. Tomorrow, I'm going to make it my priority to call Perry and ask all the questions.

"Alright, let me tell you what's going on. Then I'll grab the bottle of wine and the phone out of your bag," Ezra tells me as we sit on the couch, close enough that our knees are touching, facing one another.

"Okay." I wait to hear what he has to say with a worry deep in my soul.

"Blake did some more digging. Detective Johnson is treating this as a missing persons investigation. Blake knew in his gut something didn't sit right, a sixth sense he's always had. It seems Scotty boy has a little problem with spending as well as liking to indulge a little too much in the illegal variety of a certain drug. He's pulling bank records for all of them and has someone on Scott at all times. The other loophole Blake figured out was that Bonnie and Chad's life insurance policy, if they ever come up missing for longer than a period of time, will default the money to him. The way things are turning out, it's not looking too good. Add in the fact that your timeline matches up, something isn't sitting right. Blake can't tell the detective all he's found because it's not by the cuff. What he is doing is feeding it to a media source that will make them look harder and push deeper while his eyes are on Scott." I blink my eyes rapidly, trying to digest what I think Ezra is saying. It's hard to believe, let alone fathom. I mean, sure, Scott was a little, well, different, aloof maybe, but this is not what I expected at all.

"Are you saying what I think you're saying? That Scott made them disappear?" I gulp back a breath of air, unable to get the words out. They're too cruel to say out loud.

"I am." Ezra turns watery, as I'm unable to hold back the emotion. I've known Bonnie and Chad forever. They helped me become the person I am today, to figure out what I wanted out of life when I was floundering. They gave me a purpose in the form of a job, molding me into the hard-working person I am now, and I can't believe they could potentially not be around anymore. A sob works its way up my throat. Ezra doesn't let me fall apart alone. I'm engulfed in his arms, head in the crook of his neck, tears streaming down my face, coating my cheeks, ruining another one of Ezra's shirts, but he doesn't care.

"Let it out, sunshine. Let it out," he soothes, consoles, and coddles me in only the way Ezra can.

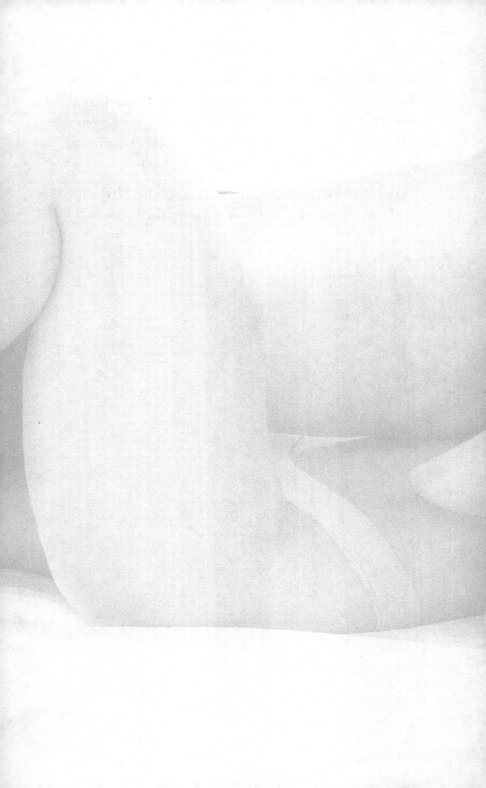

TWENTY-EIGHT

Ezra

"Go back to sleep," I tell Millie, trying to keep her ass in bed. She woke up earlier this morning, anticipating to get up and open the coffee shop. It took some time to explain to her that the shop being closed for today won't kill her. Bad pun intended and all. It took some cajoling, but she went back to sleep, probably because her body was so worn out from the crying jags and worry. She was out like a light in no time at all.

"I don't think lying around all morning is going to happen. I need to make some phone calls. If I'm not going to work, I can at least call Perry and ask him if moving in the middle of a loan process that is falling through is okay. I feel bad even making plans like this when Bonnie and Chad are missing." Yeah, this next subject is going to suck, and it's going to have her reeling.

175

"About that. You can call Perry and ask him, tell him that things are going to be slow going for a little while. He might know already." I'm going to keep Millie off her phone and the television off as much as I can. Last night was hard enough on her. It took a couple of hours to calm her down, a few glasses of wine and her talking on the phone to Vanessa for another hour, then to her grandma. Only then for the news to make an announcement of Scott's arrest at the eleven-o'clock news, catapulting her into another crying spell. It was a long time after that until she finally found sleep. It took even longer for me because as expected, with Millie's name being attached as the barista at Books and Brews, my name was being thrown out.

"I guess I'm out of a job, too." She takes a deep breath. I don't say anything. "Okay, enough of the pity party. I'm getting up and going to take a shower. If anything else bad happens today, don't tell me." She attempts to slide off me, but I hold on to her for a moment.

"You're allowed to worry about yourself, sunshine. Let's get through the week and see where things go. I'm all for you calling Perry and moving in here soon." I don't tell her that if she didn't figure it out, I'd be moving her in with me when she was out with Nessa next time.

"I know, but I still feel bad. Ugh." She drops her head, groaning.

"Love you, sunshine. Go hop in the shower. I'm going to make a few phone calls and figure out what's going on, okay?" I use my hand to lift her head up, needing her eyes on mine.

"I love you, Ezra. I'll come and find you when I'm done." My lips move to hers, sliding over them once, then twice, my tongue snaking out to lap at her lower lip for a moment.

Millicent slides out of bed. One of my shirts is covering her body. I grab my phone off the night-stand, making sure damage control is done. Luckily, I was able to turn the television off before they started talking about Scott's charges, a list the size of my arm, including hiring someone to take out his parents in a literal sense and trying to get as much money as he could. Luckily, Millie was making the deposits, and he wasn't too much of an idiot to fuck around with the business side of things. Bonnie and Chad had their account set up so a certain amount each deposit would go to their personal account, which Scott had no problem using for his gambling and coke addiction.

I pick up my phone. A text from our work group chat appears.

> Parker: Nessa is on standby. Let me know if we're needed at your place.
>
> Theo: I'm at the office. Don't come up here at all.

Boston: Fucking media frenzy is a shit show. There was no containing my shit. Sorry to leave you guys to Dickscott.

Ezra: You did me a solid. Thanks for taking that. Means Millie won't have to see the Smithers plastered on the TV, since it's all about your favorite family member.

Boston: Never a problem. New Orleans is calling my name. I'll check in later.

I close out that thread, noticing another one from Sly telling me he's doing damage control. No other words need to be said. Once the dust has settled, we'll get the ball rolling for Millie to officially own Books and Brews. It's a shit situation. I know it'll take her some time to get over their deaths and not feel guilty. No one is really a winner in this scenario, and that fucking sucks for my woman.

TWENTY-NINE

Millie

One Month Later

"ARE YOU SURE?" I ask the owner of the building Books and Brews is located in. It's been weird. One minute you're on this high where everything seems to be perfect, and the next you're feeling guilty because two innocent people lost their lives to their own son. Sadly, Bonnie and Chad's bodies were never found, even with Scott's confession. It was the one thing he wasn't willing to give the police. He's a sick piece of shit, and while their only family was in jail awaiting his trial, the community rallied, putting together a small ceremony of sorts, during which everyone said how they loved them.

"I'm positive," he tells me. *Reluctance* would be the word to describe how I'm feeling. Books and Brews has been closed since everything unfolded. It couldn't

be open for business until a whole bunch of paperwork was filed. I had the keys, but that didn't mean it
was open for customers. Instead, I'd come in twice a
week to make sure all the equipment was running and
the place was clean. It was a hard pill to swallow that
anything could happen, including me not being able
to purchase the equipment inside or keep my loan
open for this long. Perry gave me the go-ahead to
move residences. They'd have to re-run my credit
anyways, but I had to get a utility bill changed into my
name, and Ezra was not thrilled with the idea of me
paying for anything. It wasn't because I couldn't pay
it; I could. Especially since after I moved in, bills were
non-existent. Ezra was just being his alpha-man self,
wanting to pay for everything. Including the startup
costs for the papers I'm signing now.

My eyes move to Ezra's. He's sitting beside me as I
sign what feels like my life away. My loan will cover
the amount for all the equipment, furniture, and
vendor contracts that Bonnie and Chad secured. It
took a lot of work, talking, and negotiating, some of
which came with Ezra's knowledge.

"Here goes nothing." I sign my name on the dotted
line, the last piece of paper to finish transferring
everything into my name. A dream that was almost
sidetracked. Somehow managing to pull this off still
makes me want to pinch myself. One thing I know for
sure, the framed photo of Bonnie and Chad will stay
exactly where it is. I owe them so much and wish it
were them in front of me instead of a stranger.

"Congratulations." We shake hands, then he hands me a new set of keys to the front and back doors, a contingency Ezra suggested since who knew who else could have them as well.

"Thank you." He nods and sees himself out.

"Ezra, I couldn't have done all of this without you. You've been the glue holding my pieces together, my business partner in a sense, and the love of my life. I have so much to thank you for that words could barely scratch the surface." His lips are on mine almost before I finish speaking. No words are necessary; it's in the way he is there for me. Always.

Epilogue

EZRA

Six Months Later

"I CAN'T BELIEVE WE WERE ABLE TO PULL IT OFF. I mean, seriously, I get two days off a week now. I don't know if that was stupid on my part or not," Millie tells me as we walk through the coffee shop. A lot of changes have been made—paint, a new sign, more plants. A moody yet calming atmosphere is what she was going for. I'd say she nailed it with the black painted walls except behind the bar, where brick was exposed during the first two weeks Books and Brews was hers. The store had already been closed for a month, so Millie took the plunge and gave the place a face lift. Wood ceilings and dark hardwood floors pulled the coffee part together. She also invested in new tables and chairs, well, new to her. Not a table or chair matched. It worked well for her. She kept the hodgepodge of coffee mugs, an ode to Bonnie and Chad. Plus, my woman has this thing about recycling and reusing as much as she can.

"I'd say it was smart. Only having you home Sundays sucked." Today, we're doing a walk-through of the bookstore part of her baby. The shop is closed, and the carpenters have just finished staining the bookshelves. This part has been closed for a week. Millie grumbled the entire time, hating that a section was inaccessible. She has big plans in the works, and this was the last part in order to make that happen.

"On that we can agree," she responds. Hiring four baristas has helped. Sadly, Tasha had already secured a new job by the time things changed. No one could fault her; she's a college student and needed a job. Luckily, the employees she has working for her are now rock steady, don't call out, and know the ropes. No one has to make daily deposits; she has a vault they put the cash in, and Millie can deal with it the next day. Now she has the weekend off, right along with me.

"It sure would have been nice if the ladders weren't a liability. Think about all the wasted space that could have books on the top shelfs, but alas, I guess that means I'll have to go thrifting to fill in the space." She has a thing about not liking empty spaces. My once minimalist-style home has now changed, too. It doesn't bother me. The place wasn't a home; it was a house with four walls, a roof, and a view. Now it's mine and Millicent's.

While she's got her eyes on the room, her back to me, I take the ring out of my pocket. It's a platinum ring with a vintage emerald, three-quarter cut diamond. And you guessed it, I had to purchase it on a website that sold estate jewelry. She probably wouldn't mind if it was bought brand new, but knowing how Millie, I knew she'd appreciate this more.

"Millicent." I'm down on one knee, waiting for her to turn around, never thinking I'd ever be here. Where I was once against labels, girlfriend, partner, or wife, the whole damn thing wasn't appealling to me. That's changed. *I* changed. It was time, and I knew in order to save myself, it was me who had to put in the work.

"Ezra." She spins around, exasperated, my voice pulling her out of what I'm sure is a daydream of how she'll pull everything together. Until she sees me.

"Millie, there's nothing I want more in my life than for you to be my wife. Marry me?" I watch as she stands there, frozen in place, hands covering her mouth, tears spilling down her cheeks. Unable to stand it any longer, I'm off my bended knee and on my feet.

"I'm going to need your words, sunshine. Tell me you want this as much as I do." I walk us until her back is against the shelf. My hand reaches for hers, sliding the ring on as she nods her answer.

"Yes, Ezra, yes." I brush my mouth over the ring I've just placed on her left hand, loving the way a symbol I picked out is now a part of her, one that she'll never take off.

"Fuck yes. I love you, Millicent, so damn much."

"And I love you, Ezra Hudson. I can't wait to be your wife and for you to be my husband. I do have one question, though." All I want is my mouth on hers, and she's got a question.

"What's that?"

"How long does our engagement have to be?" I smile, loving that she's already thinking about the wedding.

"The shorter, the better. Kind of like the dress you're wearing right now." My hand glides up the outside of her thighs, and when I lift her up, she wraps her legs around my waist.

"Good, because I don't want to wait long. It's been long enough in my eyes. A small intimate wedding, close friends and family only?" Millicent should know I'd give her the fucking world if she wanted it.

"Sounds good to me. Eloping to Vegas would be even better. How about this weekend?" I don't give her time to answer. I'll get it later, after I kiss my fiancée, that is.

Epilogue

MILLIE

One Year Later

A WEDDING AND BECOMING PREGNANT ALL WITHIN THE past year and a half. We had a small intimate ceremony followed by a dinner at a restaurant. Neither Ezra nor I wanted anything big or over the top. All we cared about was finally being husband and wife. The honeymoon we took more than made up for what most would call lackluster for a man who's an owner of Four Brothers. We didn't care. Two weeks on an island, the sun, and the sand; it was perfection while also nerve wracking. I was worried about leaving Books and Brews even though it was well established, turning more of a profit than ever with a new event weekly—sometimes, an author does a reading with a small signing in an intimidate setting, or we hold a mic night where artists share a poem or a song. They

TORY BAKER

bring their fans, and our usuals come for something new, so everyone wins. That still didn't stop me from worrying and asking Nessa and Parker if they wouldn't mind stopping in a couple of times a week. Thankfully, they had no problem doing so, which meant Ezra and I were worry free on our honeymoon. It wasn't until five months ago that I brought up I was ready to start trying, feeling like my biological clock was ticking. Yes, I know, it wasn't. Early thirties is still considered young. The timing just felt right.

Now I'm three months pregnant. I have a slight bump that seemed to develop overnight, one that Ezra can't keep his hands off of. My day at the shop ended earlier. The employees are top notch, and while we've had baristas come and go, my manager has it going on in all the best ways. I literally go in a few hours a day, help fill the void if necessary, do the paperwork, mingle with customers, and enjoy not having to be there every waking hour.

"Hi, Mrs. Hudson," Ezra's assistant welcomes me as I step off the elevator on his floor. They each have their own floor, an assistant, and a team. Even Parker and Boston, though because Parker prefers to work from home, his assistant keeps everything moving like a well-oiled machine. Boston's the same way, except he's now in New Orleans. The guys love and hate it. They're okay with it because he's happy and no longer underneath his father's scrutinous eye. The only reason they hate is because he's not here when they feel like grabbing a drink or have an emergency meeting.

"Hi, Madeline. Is he busy?" I ask, lunch and coffee in hand, another added bonus the Books and Brews launched—pastries, muffins, and sandwiches are now added on the menu, making it easy on customers, me included, when I decide to stop in to see Ezra.

"Nope. Even if he were, you know Mr. Hudson would have me cancel whatever was going on to make time for you," she states.

"That is true, thank you." I walk past her desk, not knocking but using my elbow to open the door before Madeline can get up to help me. She does so much already. Plus, I'll have to get used to multitasking once our little one is born. I use my hip to push the door open, walk a few steps inside, use the bottom of my foot to close it, and head toward my husband. Ezra is sitting behind his desk, on the phone, a look of annoyance written on his face until his eyes lock on me. I tip my head to the side as I walk, noticing his suit jacket is off, sleeves of his shirt rolled up, which shows off his muscular forearms. It has my pregnancy hormones raging with desire.

"I don't care what it takes. Handle it. I'm not reachable for the next hour." He hangs up the phone, not waiting for an answer on the other end of the line, or that's what I'm assuming.

"Bad day?" I ask once I'm close to his desk, setting the reusable bag with our food and the cardboard carrier with Books and Brews to-go cups down, all of it recyclable, another change I ensured.

"Not anymore. This is a treat. Come here, sunshine."
He puts his phone down and pushes his chair back. I
do as I'm told, mostly because it's where I was
heading anyway. Plus, add in that tone of voice, and
I'm instantly wet and ready for him.

"I'm here. Now what are you going to do with me?" I
arch an eyebrow at him. His hands wrap around my
hips, lifting me up without him so much as moving
until I'm sitting on his desk in front of him, thighs
spread, causing the light and flowy dress to slide up.

"Oh, there's a lot I'm going to do to you, but first, I've
got someone to say hello to." Ezra does this daily, first
thing in the morning, if I see him in the middle of the
day, and always before bedtime.

"Your child is giving me heartburn today. Do you
think you could talk to him? I could really use a
morning of not having to drink apple cider vinegar."
Nothing else works. Milk, which is gross, but it was
worth a shot, and antacids didn't touch it. The only
thing that did was apple cider vinegar, which is gross,
too, but desperate times call for desperate measures.

"I'll see what I can do." With that, he moves his hands
away from my hips and slides them to the hem of my
dress, because Ezra only talks to our boy when my
stomach is bare. I lift one hip up, then the other until
I'm gathering the fabric with my hands as more skin is
bared to his watchful gaze. "Christ, Millicent, I'll
never get used to this. Seeing you like this, watching
our child grown inside of you, it's fucking awe inspir-
ing." He moves his chair, widening my thighs even

further, and takes a deep breath, sure as shit smelling the desire that only he can awaken. My eyes watch as my husband dips his head and places a kiss on my stomach. "Hey, bud, you being good to your mom? Try to simmer down on the heartburn for me. Kissing her after she drinks that crazy concoction is weird as shit." He places another peck on my stomach.

"Ezra." He tips his head up to look into my eyes.

"I'm going to have my dessert first, sunshine." And I'm not going to deny my husband, especially when what I crave all the time is him.

Want more Billionaire Playboys? Playing With Her, Boston's story is coming April 16th!

Amazon

Coming Next

A Courting Curves romance is coming March 6th!

Tempting the Judge

Amazon

Chapter One
Eden

I look in the full-length mirror I have propped up in my walk-in closet, the true selling point in my condo because let me tell you the bedrooms are teeny tiny, to the point where the only thing that fits in my bedroom is a queen-sized bed and two nightstands on either side, not even a dresser could fit anywhere in the postage stamp of a room. The second bedroom is a makeshift office-library, more for books than work any day of the week, I do enough of that well at the work.

My golden colored hair is perfectly in place, an inverted low bun, upswept hairstyle, not a lock of hair out of place, it can't be a hindrance while at work. The understated make up I put on took me less than ten minutes to do, the majority of that time was spent on my eye lashes, curling them, coating them in a thick layer of mascara, taking breaks in between and switching out different brands of tubes as well. A pair of pearl earrings are adorning my first hole, leaving the second hole empty, this is the work dressed Eden, not the hanging out with friends Eden. Those are two completely different people, business oriented versus the thirty-year-old that lets her hair down, drinks a few too many beers, and has no problem staying up or out well past three o'clock in the morning or I should say that was myself, until a few months ago. Now I'm caught in a tidal wave of emotions, the ups and downs of what not to do and I've got a list that plays on repeat in my head.

Things not to do:

1- *Don't fall for your boss that's fifteen years older than you.*

2- *Don't touch your boss.*

3- *Don't have sex with your boss.*

4- *Don't have a threesome with your boss and your boss's friend.*

5- *Don't engage in said behavior in the judge's chamber with the judge you work with and his friend who just so happens to be the bailiff.*

Except that's what I did, that's what I continue to keep doing, and while I know it's illicit, will explode like a grenade in a war-torn country, shrapnel not giving a shit who it hurts in its wake, I won't put a stop to it either, honestly, I can't. The forbidden has never tasted so good, it's like blood running through your veins and the air you so desperately need to breathe.

I turn my thoughts back to getting ready, knowing what will happen if I'm late for Judge Kavanaugh's court hearing, I'll be in even more trouble, and not in the dock your pay, receiving a written or verbal warning. That's not his way, and while I make sure my black blouse is tucked into my white midi skirt, the whole outfit is tight fitting and hugging my curves in all the sinful ways stopping at my calves and is exactly what Kavanaugh prefers. A full body quiver works its way down my spine thinking about the note he sent me late last night along with a package, inside was a gold and nude color confection, hand beaded floral embroidery to cover my nipples, other than that it was entirely see through, the softest material that has probably ever touched my skin, the low slung thong matching in color and sheerness, leaving nothing to the imagination, thankfully my standing wax appointment keeps me completely bare, otherwise it would pull away from the effect, completely. The only bad thing is if Kavanaugh so much as looks at me, I'm toast, the panties are so miniscule, I'm sure to leave a wetness in my wake. I turn away, knowing if I keep thinking about any and all things Judge Samuel Kavanaugh, I'll never make it out of here, my eyes peruse the plethora of heels I have in my closet, walking in them isn't hard, especially for the short amount of time I'm on my feet, wearing the highest heel for what it does to my ass, legs, and stature is what I'm after. You know what they say, beauty is pain. My hand reaches for the way too expensive red bottom soles, a splurge I gave to myself after saving for nearly a year, black patent leather, timeless, and pulling this outfit together entirely. One last look in the mirror, then I'm heading out of my closet, grabbing my bag that carries everything I could possibly need for work.

"Phone, check. Keys, check. Sunglasses, check. Bag, check," I say, going through another checklist, this one out loud instead of in my head. I'm a list queen, written down, electronically, it doesn't matter I use them in any way possible. I'm just putting my sunglasses on, keys in hand to lock the front door when my phone buzzes. I glance down, a worry settling in my stomach in case it's mom or dad texting this early in the morning, if that's the case it could only mean something is wrong. Thankfully, I'm wrong and it's a certain man that plagues my thoughts night and day.

Judge: Baby girl, my Chambers, thirty minutes, I'll be checking.

His text shouldn't make my nipples pebble or my core clench, being told what to do should be a major turn off, it's not, at least for me it isn't.

Millie: And if I didn't do as I'm told?

Judge: My hand will be meeting your ass, over and over again.

I don't respond, that's an answer enough from him, needing to get my butt moving, already pushing it. The last time Kavanaugh doled out a punishment it was not easy to sit for the rest of the day, though the orgasm he gave me afterwards made it completely worth it. He may be fifteen years my senior, a man of authority, dominating in bed, a complete and total hot shot of a Judge, commanding a room with one look, and I'm the one he wants.

Amazon

About the Author

Tory Baker is a mom and dog mom, living on the coast of sunny Florida where she enjoys the sun, sand, and water anytime she can. Most of the time you can find her outside with her laptop, soaking up the rays while writing about Alpha men, sassy heroines, and always with a guaranteed happily ever after.

Sign up to receive her **Newsletter** for all the latest news!

Tory Baker's Readers is where you see and hear all of the news first!

Also by Tory Baker

Men in Charge

Make Her Mine

Staking His Claim

Billionaire Playboys

Playing Dirty

Playing with Fire

Vegas After Dark Series

All Night Long

Late Night Caller

One More Night

About Last Night

One Night Stand

Hart of Stone Family

Tease Me

Hold Me

Kiss Me

Please Me

Touch Me

Feel Me

Diamondback MC Second Gen.

Obsessive

Seductive

Addictive

Protective

Deceptive

Diamondback MC

Dirty

Wild

Bare

Wet

Filthy

Sinful

Wicked

Thick

Bad Boys of Texas

Harder

Bigger

Deeper

Hotter

Faster

Hot Shot Series

Fox

Cruz

Jax

Saint

Getting Dirty Series

Serviced (Book 1)

Primed (Book 2)

Licked (Book 3)

Hammered (Book 4)

Nighthawk Security

Never Letting Go (Easton and Cam's story)

Claiming Her (Book 1)

Craving More (Book 2)

Sticky Situations (Travis and Raelynn's story)

Needing Him (Book 3)

Only His (Book 4)

Carter Brothers Series

Just One Kiss

Just One Touch

Just One Promise

Finding Love Series

A Love Like Ours

A Love To Cherish

A Love That Lasts

Stand Alone Titles

Nailed

Going All In

What He Wants

Accidental Daddy

Love Me Forever

Gettin' Lucky

It's Her Love

Meant To Be

Breaking His Rules

Can't Walk Away

Carried Away

In Love With My Best Friend

Must Be Love

Sweet As Candy

Falling For Her

All Yours

Sweet Nothings Book 3—Tory Baker

Loving The Mountain Man

Crazy For You

Trick— The Kelly Brothers

Friend Zoned

His Snow Angel

223 True Love Ln.

Hard Ride

Slow Grind

1102 Sugar Rd.

The Christmas Virgin

Taking Control

Unwrapping His Present

Acknowledgments

Thank you for being here, reading, not just my books but any Author's stories. We do appreciate you more than you know, the reason why we can live out our dream is for readers, bloggers, bookstagrammers, bookmakers, Authors, and everyone in between. THANK YOU!

To my kids: A & A without you I'd be a shell of myself. You helped me find myself in a moment of darkness. Thank you for picking up the slack around the house while I was knee deep in this deadline, cooking, cleaning, and taking care of Remi (our big lug of a Weimaraner). I love you to infinity times infinity.

Amie: Seriously, we don't see each other near enough. Miss you tons!

Jordan: Oh my lanta, the hand holding, the me calling you hysterically crying or laughing, day or night, good or bad. I love you bigger than outer space. If it weren't for you pushing me to write, to see the potential in me, I wouldn't be here.

Mayra: My sprinting partner extraordinaire. Girl-friend, we made it through 2022 ahead of schedule. One day I will fly my butt to California to hug you!

Julia: How do you deal with me and my extra sprinkling of commas? The real MVP, the one who deals with my scatterbrained self, missing deadlines, rescheduling like crazy, and the person I live vicariously through social media.

All this to say, I am and will always be forever grateful, love you all!